THE JOURNEY HOME
AND OTHER STORIES

Persephone Book Nº 124
Published by Persephone Books Ltd 2017

Preface © Philip Hensher/Afterword © Valerie Waterhouse

This selection consists of five stories each from
Frost in April (1929), *No Luggage* (1930), *Five for Silver* (1932),
Honeymoon & Other Stories (1934) in the order they
appeared in the original volumes.

Endpapers taken from a 1933 textile design by Stanley Wilkinson,
a student at Bradford School of Art who lived in Keighley.

Typeset in ITC Baskerville by
Keystroke, Wolverhampton

Printed and bound in Germany by
GGP Media GmbH, Poessneck

978 191 0263 143

Persephone Books Ltd
59 Lamb's Conduit Street
London WC1N 3NB
020 7242 9292

www.persephonebooks.co.uk

THE JOURNEY HOME
AND OTHER STORIES

by

MALACHI WHITAKER

with a new preface by

PHILIP HENSHER

and afterwords by the author and

VALERIE WATERHOUSE

PERSEPHONE BOOKS
LONDON

CONTENTS

PREFACE

Not many authors are absolutely unique: almost all have a context and a web of influences. 'Malachi' Whitaker is not like other authors. Her career is exceedingly strange in its shape, and her work quite unlike anything else. She gathered no followers and was almost forgotten in her later, silent years. Reading her now, it is inexplicable how English letters failed to find a place for a writer of such verve, colour, range and power. She is one of the great English short story writers, and her work is slowly reaching some prominence.

She was born Marjorie Taylor in 1895, one of eleven children of a Yorkshire bookbinder. The social setting is exact: a craftsman of dignity, with a relationship to the work of the mind. Marjorie wrote copiously when young, including an autobiography and a complete novel, the manuscript of which fell from a Channel steamer. By this time she was married, to a businessman, Leonard Whitaker. They moved around a good deal, including living in a tent, rooms in a farmhouse, a home in an attic, and a period in Rouen. After the war, they returned to Yorkshire, and Malachi Whitaker began to write seriously. It is a Yorkshirewoman's voice, apparently direct, straight-faced in humour and tragedy, confident of its own reach and power. She needed the place she came from.

The first story she wrote, 'Sultan Jekker', awoke the interest of John Middleton Murry at the Adelphi, who published a dozen of her stories. In 1929 she published her first collection, *Frost in April*. It was well enough received to find an American publisher. Three more collections followed. Then near silence apart from a very strange autobiography, *And So Did I* (1939). Only a very few short stories have been unearthed from journals in the remaining decades of her life – she died in 1976.

Why did she fall silent? The atmosphere of the later 1930s was not quite right for her. She was from the North, but not much like Walter Greenwood, who wrote the successful *Love on the Dole* (1933). 'Northern' meant 'working class' to the English literary world then, as now: the existence and power of the Yorkshire gentry, the myriad social gradations between unemployed millworkers and Castle Howard, were a mystery to Bloomsbury. Her subjects were domestic, but not elegantly refined like Katherine Mansfield. She had an original approach to form, but could hardly be described as a radical or experimental writer. Most of all, she was changeable, and can still bewilder a reader. Her sales were always small – between 800 and 1300 copies per volume. Her publisher, Jonathan Cape, seems to have been supportive to the end, but she may just have concluded that not many people were interested. It is a sadly premature conclusion to an exceedingly interesting body of work.

The short story had long been a useful way for writers somewhat outside the metropolitan swing of things to make a mark. Even in the nineteenth century, women writers, working class writers, writers from immigrant communities had found that an editor could be quite ready to use their contributions. A curious editor like Middleton Murry was the perfect person to put a writer like Malachi Whitaker into print, and his imprimatur would encourage a publisher like Cape to take a punt on publishing collections by her. The encouragement is initially strong, but it is not necessarily very solid. Another woman writer of short stories of the time, Dorothy Edwards, had a much worse fate: her exquisite writing was first championed by David Garnett and Bloomsbury, but when he started to find her personally difficult, the merit seemed to disappear from her work. She threw herself under a train in 1934.

Support for the short story was easy to come by: how limited that support might be could soon become apparent. It's hard to know why, exactly, Malachi Whitaker stopped writing, but it's fairly clear that nobody much noticed when she did. Waves of literary fashion must have swept over her. John Middleton Murry's *Adelphi* became a magazine with an explicitly socialist agenda by 1930, setting the tone for much 1930s writing. It's difficult, too, to see the reassured reader of H E Bates's rural idylls enjoying her lucidly precise sketches. Her contemporaries, trying to place her, described her as 'the Bradford Chekhov'. It's only accurate if you remember Chekhov's occasional freakish sense of humour as well as his rich ambiguity of feeling. Another comparison might be with

Hardy, who had no hesitation in using grotesque coincidences to illuminate a situation. In his stories, as in Malachi Whitaker's, we often feel that these events could never have happened before, unsure whether it is the cruelty of existence or the cruelty of a writer supervising these events. But these influences, if they were influences, were out of fashion in the world of the 1930s and, certainly, the 1940s. Whatever happened to Malachi Whitaker, the literary world hardly missed her.

I first came across her in A S Byatt's *Oxford Book of English Short Stories* (1998), which includes her 'Landlord of the Crystal Fountain', and well remember the intangible feeling of mild confusion on reading that story. Had the thing happened which the story had said had happened? The heroine stumbles across a party of pub landlords in a train carriage, who finally nominate one of their number to marry her. It strangely reminded me of a story in Quentin Crisp's *The Naked Civil Servant*, of Crisp finding himself joyfully surrounded by a group of sailors during a trip to Portsmouth, passed from one to another. Malachi Whitaker's story had an aura of unreality, paradoxically, because such things don't usually happen in fiction. In reality, parties of pub landlords are there all the time. I tracked down what collections I could find, and discovered that the air of mild but decisive confusion arising from clear and direct statement was rather characteristic. Years later, I found myself in a restaurant next to a party of twelve men, highly similar in appearance but unplaceable, and asked them who they were: they were prosperous Swedish builders, on a whisky-tasting holiday together. They did it every year. I thought of Malachi Whitaker, and what a story she would have made of that.

Like many of the best short story writers, she is fascinated by the ordinary. Just as in Chekhov, the banal dissolves under her precise gaze, to be replaced by the unique, the freshly experienced. These things happen all the time: and yet these things have never happened before. Her stories explore, with an eager gleam, ordinary people in extraordinary situations. She loves embarrassment, that unstoppable response when things go wrong. A romantic young man sees the girl he loves approaching. He, however, is a plumber's assistant, and is inconveniently carrying a lavatory on his shoulder ('The Apprentice'). What he does, and what her polite and real reaction to his absurd solution is, forms a ripe episode, where our speculation about the future runs riotously forward. Ingenious but inappropriate solutions to difficult situations are often the cause of strange tenderness in Malachi Whitaker. A simple couple in 'Salem Street' get drunk for the first time ('"My word, Nellie," he said suddenly, "but I *have* big feet."'). They decide that the visit they have paid earlier that day, to the wife's rich brother, left some social inquiries unfulfilled, and must return to ask after wife and children. The consequences are splendidly embarrassing. But no one can doubt where the author's sympathies lie.

She is a paradoxical writer of empathetic asperity, seeming to judge and forgive in the same breath. A spinster thinks of putting herself out in order to meet a man, but in the end comes to an unusual solution when the man proves a great bore. She will have a happy, though unconventional life ('Miss

Creech of Redemouth'). When rapture comes, it comes with real radiance. Only at the very end of the beautiful 'Honeymoon' does a darker thought intrude on this unique, shared, unrepeatable bliss, and it is like a shadow in sunlight. Often suffering comes paired with a flavour of the fairy tale. The great 'Pin's Fee Wife' opens in a satisfying, comforting way: 'The three sons of the fishmonger Gabitass were dark and queer, and nobody knew them at all well.' Soon a down-trodden and mistreated skivvy is added to the mix. But this is about as much a fairy tale as *King Lear*, and Effie Shepp's suffering is real and unredeemable. There is no fairy god-mother here. Fifty years before Angela Carter's *The Bloody Chamber*, Whitaker was finding what suffering was present in the patterns of folk narrative, what could not be fixed by the assertion of a happy ending.

Like many other women writers, Malachi Whitaker was very interested by children, and many of her best stories are from a child's point of view. In one, 'For a Small Moment', the children are allowed an orgy of chaos and mess, unsupervised: the reason they go unpunished on the grown-ups' return only emerges at the end. In many of the best, a child is trying to make sense of the world – the beautiful 'The White Line' is a ménage whose relations, behaviour and limits are a puzzle to their young visitor, and also to us. The subject is so congenial to Malachi Whitaker because making sense of the world is her challenge, too. Her characters are constantly fretting about the right thing to do: frequently trying to work out how they should respond to circumstances. Sometimes they are children; sometimes simple people of narrow experience;

sometimes ordinary people who are making sense of the first days of marriage, or a first trip to Paris. In the story that initially awoke a publisher's interest, the splendidly over-eventful 'Sultan Jekker', everyone is working out whether it is possible for three people to live in sexual intimacy with each other. Jekker, Caroline and Phoebe might as well be children, trying to understand what marriage is.

The determination to regard the ordinary as extraordinary, and the extraordinary with plainness, encouraged Whitaker to write stories of completely unprecedented shapes and forms. Tucked away in her four volumes are stories consisting of two juxtaposed episodes, sixty years apart; stories that take place in the short interval between a retired tradesman falling from a high hotel window and his death; stories that begin in a dull suburban train carriage in which, we finally discover, everyone is actually dead. But even in stories with a superficially more conventional surface, the deeper structure can be disconcertingly innovative. 'Thunder Shower' takes on a very topical subject, the difficulties of procuring an abortion, but its real subject is, surely, the evasions and irrelevancies circling at increasing distances from the fact of the matter. Weather, the smell of rubber, the colours of the coats on display, all occupy a place of not-mentioning, like the conversations, never coming to the point. What we are talking about is a sexual act; but the story is an extravaganza of evasion and verbal absences.

The short story was the perfect vehicle for Whitaker's gifts, and for her particular subject. The world's oddities are glimpsed in a flash, and we pass on, partly enlightened, amused or startled. Whitaker is a writer of quick inspiration, impatience, freakish amusement and abrupt outbursts of mood; she very much likes things that have never happened before, and will never happen again. Quite often, we don't quite know how to take her. It isn't clear why she stopped writing short stories when her last collection, *Honeymoon & Other Stories*, is so excellent. Perhaps the nervous uncertainty her writing engenders in the reader was, from the point of view of the writer's desk, hard to distinguish from indifference.

But she is a unique and daring writer, whose work richly rewards exploration and rediscovery. Under her intense, scrupulous gaze, the event that happens all the time and the event that is happening only once are, in the logic of art, strangely identical. Honeymoons happen all the time: this honeymoon is happening for the first time, and will never happen again. The particular happiness, the peculiar occurrence is her subject; her voice unmistakably her own; the body of work soon over.

Philip Hensher
Geneva, 2017

THE JOURNEY HOME
AND OTHER STORIES

THE JOURNEY HOME

The girl in the corner seat noticed the rabbit without a white bob to its tail, because she had never seen a rabbit without that mark before. She had seized on the rabbit, or anything else that offered itself outside the window, to avoid looking at the face of the woman opposite, a face so ravaged by one passion or another that it was almost obscene.

She wished that the woman could have sat in another part of the train, then she could not have seen that puce-pink skull, with light – nearly white – hair running thinly out of it, nor the fat-lidded, pale green eyes, nor the crooked mouth, still more deformed by a gathered swelling in its upper left-hand corner, nor any of the innumerable harsh creases which caused the loose skin to sag more heavily. As if conscious of her own defects, the woman kept smiling a wide, propitiatory, nervous smile, showing an even row of cream-coloured false teeth.

There was a honeymoon couple in the carriage, who had spent all of their seaside holiday dancing in stifling, third-rate ballrooms, and were now going back to their furnished rooms, knowing that a successful holiday lay just behind them, and that they were journeying towards another one, only a year ahead. They had already booked lodgings for next year. Before the carriage had filled, the young husband had entertained everybody by extolling the great cleverness of his bride. With many years' experience of seaside landladies, this young woman had bought her butter in an oblong shape, which she ostentatiously measured off after every meal, to the alleged chagrin of the landlady. Both bride and groom were dark, pert, and good-looking. They sat in opposite corners, but rarely looked at each other, addressing their remarks to the other people.

The train was crowded, but there was only one man standing in this carriage. He was long and thin, with a moustache like six or seven pieces of old string hanging over his upper lip. After he was tired of standing, his wife stood up, let him sit in her place, then without a glance around, sat on his long, bony knees. They were very quiet, never spoke at all, and looked dull and prim. One wondered why they had been to Summersea, why they had married, and so back to why they had been born.

There was also a fat woman who had arrived late, and had not got enough room. She threw many indignant glances left and right, with no effect. She had to sit a little forward all the time, and snorted continually, 'hn, hn'. She kept her gloves on, as if they were the outward sign of inward superiority, and would not join in the general conversation, which, as the journey grew, gradually diminished. Eventually everybody whispered in twos, or was silent. Only the sound of some younglings singing in the carriage next door brought fugitive smiles to faces here and there. The woman with the green eyes smoothed down her untidy hair with an incredibly large red hand, which she brought suddenly out of her green coat pocket.

The girl yawned with weariness and heat. The windows were down, but the air was stagnant; even the rushing train did not seem to cause any disturbance in the atmosphere. There was still over an hour's journey to be made. Soon the toy town of Bell Banning, all red roofs and green trees, would come into sight.

She had taken off her hat, and placed a blue silk handkerchief behind her head as a barrier between her shining hair and the dusty red-padded back of the seat. Her face was pale, her skin slightly roughened by the strong sea air to which she was unaccustomed, save for a week or two each year. Her eyes, a mixture of blue and hazel, were expressive, thickly lashed. A few buff-coloured freckles showed palely on her cheekbones and over the bridge of her nose.

Her husband, on her left, was looking up at the dirty-white roof of the compartment. She noticed that his hair needed cutting. It was curling into his neck in a manner she did not like. Yet she saw that he appeared much better for the change. He had a thin, clear skin, which tanned easily, so that now he looked healthy and strong.

She began to think that they ought to come to the seaside more often. They should be able to afford it, and nearly all the year round there were cheap fares. But the new house took up so much money, there was something to buy each month for it, and the Building Society to pay, and rates to put by, electricity to reckon. As soon as they thought all was clear, something would give out, and have to be replaced. When they did manage to save a little money, it was needed for things more urgent than holidays. They had no children as yet, and wanted them spasmodically, when they saw the pretty little dressed-up things on the promenade. They loved and admired each other very much, had been married for seven years, and rarely disagreed. They were very happy, and conscious of their happiness.

Her husband had drawn her hand through the crook of his arm, and she turned and smiled at him as he squeezed her fingers. Though it was hot, she liked to feel her hand inside his, safe. It made her feel one with him. She thought that the fresh tan of his complexion suited him, and that his eyes were brighter. He liked to be outdoors. Much of his time he spent in the garden of the new house. It was a large plot of ground, and he was cultivating a small piece at a time. He wanted to have a beautiful garden for his old age, and was filling it with plants and trees.

As the train rushed through Bell Banning station, with its well-cared-for flower beds glowing under the afternoon sun, she shut her eyes. After all, though the holiday had been nice, she was looking forward to her home again, the tiny kitchen where she cooked Saul's breakfast every morning, grilling bacon, cooking an egg over the light and browning toast below it; brewing tea, and putting the teapot on the hearth with the cosy over it, and stopping, even so early in the day, to kiss the back of Saul's head as he kneeled down, lighting the fire; running away laughing, as he turned to clasp her knees, and telling him she hadn't a minute to spare, so that he had to run after her and say that it didn't matter a hang if all the bacon in the world was burnt to bits so long as she loved him.

She thought of the pretty sitting room, which looked away across the valley, and from the windows of which she liked to watch the heavy blue-grey clouds of showery days, or the bright star show of windy nights.

The train drew to a standstill. She forgot the woman opposite, who had pulled on a green hat which covered her pink skull. Somehow, she was on the platform and through the barrier. Everybody was silent, it was not a noisy crowd, such as one would have expected a holiday crowd to be. The shuffling sound of shoe-leather against stone rose but faintly. It seemed curiously dim in the station. She clung to Saul's arm, and walked out into the familiar square. Here, also, it was strangely silent. She noticed that there was very little traffic about, but she felt stiff and tired, and was glad to climb into the tram that would take them home.

Their house was almost at the terminus, and stood on a slight rise, about half a mile away. They always went to the top of the tram, and when they were nearly home, the house seemed to be riding towards them. She noticed that the tram was running very quietly, that nobody came to collect their fares, that they were the only passengers.

All at once she became filled with fear, and to calm herself, looked for the little house. It came riding towards them, perched on its ledge of hill, its windows smiling a reassuring welcome. She marked the tiny bushes which were one day to be great trees, the small winding paths which led from one tilled patch to another, and the untidy stretches of weed-grown greenery which Saul had not yet had time to dig.

Again, panic fear enveloped her. It ought not to be so dark, yet giant purple clouds bellied in a canopy overhead. She turned towards her husband, groping for contact with his warm, loving hand, not understanding the terrible dread which pressed her down. He was not with her. Her frantic gaze could not pierce the gathering gloom. The clouds seemed to swoop and overwhelm her. She looked down at her own familiar hands, her knees, her feet. They, too, were gone.

By that time, the express had collided with the excursion train, just outside Bell Banning station, and the girl in the corner was already dead.

SULTAN JEKKER

A fat man, with loose, light-pink cheeks, was sitting on the side of a flat truck, eating his lunch. He had a torn gabardine raincoat on, and a cap so shrunken by rain that it made his face look enormous. His legs, which were short, did not reach the ground as he sat, and his feet hung inertly, toes pointing inwards. He faced the blank wall of a newly-stuccoed tram-shed, and ate slowly and with a vague sadness from some thick slices of white bread wrapped in newspaper.

He was not alone, there being four or five other men also on the truck, seated around it facing east, north, and west. They discussed starting-prices as they ate, and interlaced their exchange of news with loud and careless oaths. They did not trouble to lower their voices if a woman passed, which was not infrequently; and none of the corporation employees, hurrying in and out of the tram-shed like preoccupied ants, interfered with, or spoke to them. They were navvies, and had come out into the sunlight to eat.

Suddenly the fat man, whose name was Clarence Waterman, gave a loud shout, and said in a surprised, angry voice, 'The bitches! They said they would put some meat in.'

He had just discovered that he was eating only bread, but his companions took no notice of him. It often happened this way. The big man lived with two women, who were for ever quarrelling and fighting over him, and sometimes they forgot altogether, in the bitterness of their early morning disputes, to put up any lunch at all for him. He swore he would beat them on his return home, but nearly always he forgot. His companions, who for some reason of their own called him 'Jekker', were proud of him, as they were all married, and thought of him and his two women with envy.

However, he was not to be envied. These women had come strangely into his life, and had as strangely stayed there, without his consent. They were violently jealous and frequently injured each other, their faces rarely remaining for a week free from marks of intense conflict. Before their coming, he had had peace. He had lived alone in an isolated cottage for fifteen years of his adult life, and at the age of thirty-five, within a fortnight, these two women, strangers, were living in the utmost intimacy with him and each other.

Phoebe, the elder, was a raddled blonde of about forty, with stout, flat feet, on which she wore men's boots, but no stockings. She sold lavender, also peppermint cordial, which she made herself with essence and questionable water from the well behind the cottage. When these were out of season she hawked bootlaces. She had an impudent and ingratiating manner, and a certain hard stare with which to terrorise timid housewives. She was without a moral standard and had few womanly virtues. The first time she called at Jekker's cottage with her lavender and her cordial, she opened the door after repeated knockings to find the man seated on the hearth with a red shawl twisted around his head, groaning with toothache. Before he could stop her, she had pulled the aching tooth with one turn of her large brown finger and thumb. Later in the evening, she took him down to the inn, and stayed with him until he drank himself insensible. Then she alternately pushed and carried him home, picking him up as he fell. Once arrived, she pulled off his boots and drove him before her into the bedroom. He accepted her without surprise, as a fortnight later he accepted Caroline.

It was really Phoebe who invited Caroline to live with them. They met her at the Vine Leaf, the squalid house they patronised. She picked rags 'on piece', and drank to forget her husband, who, through miscalculation, would have to spend the next three years in gaol. She had reached the maudlin stage, and quiet tears were running endlessly down her cheeks when the inn-frequenters trooped out, disturbing the starry night, rapt with autumn silence. Phoebe, big with beer-engendered kindliness, was comforting her, saying, 'Don't cry, lass, there's many a better man, many a better man – ' The usually cautious Phoebe had had too much to drink, and was finding the way with difficulty. Jekker lingered, but she did not care, as she knew he had left the door-key under a stone.

Somehow she reached the cottage with Caroline, Jekker following. The long walk up the hill, the cart-ruts frozen hard and the tufted grass already white with rime, the complacent crow of an awakened rooster, they did not hear, see, or feel. All they wanted was further oblivion. Phoebe said that Caroline could sleep on the big horsehair couch in the kitchen before the fire. Jekker, stumbling in, lit the smelly paraffin lamp without accident, began to poke the fire which had been made up ready for their return, forgot, let the poker fall from his hand, and sprawled across a wooden chair, snoring a little in drunken stupor. Phoebe, on the horsehair couch destined for the rag-woman, was already fast asleep, her long, unlovely mauve-coloured lips hanging apart, and wisps of her light hair moving with each breath.

Caroline, slightly over thirty, dark, red-faced, in a stained, greeny-black dress, passed the back of her hand over her smeared face, and broke again into low sobbing. The noise awoke Jekker, who stared at her bemused, and then said in a beseeching voice, 'Now, Ca'line; now, Ca'line.' He had opened his small, dull eyes to their full extent, and his mouth looked like a red-plush button in the middle of his great face. The woman did not appear to find anything humorous about him, for she returned his stare long minutes, the tears lying unheeded on her red cheeks, and no others appearing to take their place. It was Phoebe alone who spent the night on the horsehair couch.

In the morning, the rage of the older woman was dreadful to see. The first of the endless fights took place, then tears of exhaustion, then a surly reconciliation. The man watched with apathetic looks. It was not his affair. They should fight it out, and let the best woman win.

It was not long before everything settled into routine. At first, the women stayed in the house the day long, not daring to go out, in fear of being locked out, but after furtive essays, expeditions to the yard and the well, they began to trust each other a little. Each wanted a home, a man. They also wanted food and drink, and as early on Jekker would not give them any money, they had to go out and earn some. The lavender-woman had no set times for working, and this would sometimes exasperate Caroline, who laboured for fixed hours, though on piece-work.

They passed the long winter evenings, when they did not drink, in making a rug of cloth pieces, which Caroline stole and brought home under her skirt. They had nothing to say, so they did not talk. The orange light from the lamp illumined the low-ceiled room with its two heavy beams. A square table, covered with brown linoleum, stood in the middle of the room. The couch, two or three wooden chairs, and a small, painted, wooden dresser was the extent of the furniture. There was nothing on the walls but a grocer's almanac of twenty years ago, going yellow and turning inwards in spite of the four rusty tacks which held it in place.

Phoebe had a secret passion for cosmetics, and would spend her spare pence on beautifiers, which gave her a grim and ugly look. She only used them when she wished to appear seductive before her unresponsive lord. Sometimes during the evening, Phoebe would steal upstairs and come down after a while with rouge and powder on her hard, lined, impudent face, her hair grotesquely frizzled, and even crimson smears on her light-coloured lips. As soon as she opened the doorway at the bottom of the stairs, Caroline would break into ribald sneers. 'Come in, you beauty, you!' she would shout, along with other remarks, but Phoebe would not take the slightest notice of her, beyond a whispered, 'Get out,' which command, curiously enough, the younger woman sooner or later always obeyed. Phoebe felt that, by right of priority, she ought occasionally to have the man to herself. Caroline did not care, as she was only existing until her own man came out of prison, yet often she stole the helpless prey successfully from out of the very hands of the older woman.

Jekker began to hate Phoebe, with her light-blue eyes, pulled down at the corners, and her flabby, creased cheeks, daubed clumsily with rank powder, with her attempts at coquetry, which the stolid, animal-like man did not understand. He preferred the buoyant Caroline, and began to follow her with his round, flat eyes, and to look to her for help, and to keep her in with appealing motions of his heavy arms when she would prepare to go out and leave him alone with Phoebe.

He wished that Phoebe would go, but he knew that she would not, and he had not the wit to devise a means of making her leave. Sometimes he locked the door on her, and kept her out all night, but she was always waiting in the yard, shouting and screaming from early dawn, and clawing for Caroline's face as soon as the younger woman came out, yawning, and twisting her straggling black hair with exaggerated nonchalance. He never locked Caroline out.

Over two years passed in strange companionship. As if they had been one real wife, he put money down each week on the brown-covered table, and let them buy food for him. At first, each had eaten separately, but they found it cheaper to share. So now he sat on the truck, and grumbled because his women had forgotten to put the meat he had paid for between his slices of bread.

His bread finished, and the last of the cold tea drunk from the dark-blue enamel can, he jumped down and stood morosely looking over the green landscape. A thin film spread over the face of the sun, and a whipping shower stung his face and made his cheeks quiver. The sky filled with low clouds and heavier, steadier rain began to fall. The navvies looked around. Perhaps they would be rained off, but they had already put a morning's work in, so they did not mind. After being dismissed, they tramped off sturdily, in twos or alone.

Jekker stumped along by himself. His legs were slightly bowed, as if bent by the massive body above them. He had buttoned his raincoat high, and walked with lowered head fronting the rain, the blue tea-can creaking in his right hand, thinking about Caroline, whom he liked, and Phoebe, whom he didn't like. An idea had come into his head that if he were to lock Phoebe out every night, say for a month, she would surely begin to realise that she was not wanted. He might try. Meanwhile, he climbed the hill to his home.

Phoebe was in the kitchen when he arrived, humming to herself and smiling in a secret way. She made him some tea, which he did not want, so he pushed the mug away and sat staring into the newly-lit fire. Then he pulled a plug of tobacco from his pocket, cut off some small pieces, rubbed them between his hands, and finally lit his pipe with a smouldering coal.

'Rained off?' casually enquired Phoebe, after an hour's silence.

He did not think it worth while to reply, in view of the rain which was now beating forcefully against the small window. Phoebe was engaged in washing his shirt and socks, a job which usually fell to Caroline.

Evening drew in earlier because of the rain. Still Phoebe moved about, the secret smile widening her wide mouth. She prepared the evening meal, for two.

'Where's Ca'line?' asked the man, breaking his afternoon's silence.

'How should I know?' parried Phoebe, but there was a laugh, a sound of triumph in her rough voice, which penetrated even the dull brain of Jekker, and made him look at her with eyes towards the surface of which some faint expression struggled.

They ate and drank noisily. After the meal, Phoebe cleared away and put the things into a cupboard. Then she turned the drying shirt and socks and things of her own that were airing near the fire. The evening wore away, ticked towards night by the tin alarm clock on the mantelshelf.

'There was no meat in them samwidges today, again,' said Jekker, taking a knife from his pocket and scraping around the bowl of his pipe with it. He flushed darkly. He had decided that Phoebe needed a lesson, and that he would give her one. The omission was probably her fault. He would give her a hiding, and have her crying when Caroline came in. That would please Caroline. He wondered where she was. His face was set in its usual expressionless mask, except for the shadow of a frown over his eyes. Throwing his knife on to the table, he rose unwillingly. Phoebe had disappeared.

In five minutes she came down the stairway, first her big, patched boots, then her dirty dress, then her large, coarse face plastered with make-up. She paused at the bottom of the steps to look at herself once more in the oblong, tin-framed mirror she had herself bought and hung there. As she turned, the man met her with a blow on the face.

'That'll learn yer not to put meat in my samwidges,' he roared.

The woman flared up with rage, and swore at him.

'It was Ca'line put 'em up,' she shouted, dodging another blow, and as he pursued her around the kitchen, striking at her with his ham-like hands, she yelled, 'An' it's the last food Ca'line'll ever put up for you, yer – '

He caught hold of her stringy hair, and held her. 'Wot d'yer mean by that?' he asked, his huge face suffused with blood.

She twisted until she could look up at him out of her angry, downward-turning eyes. 'Wot do I mean by that?' she mocked him, 'I mean she'll never come back 'ere, the bloody, pinchin' 'ellcat! I've seen to that!'

For a minute he held her by the hair and arms, while he thought. Not for a second of the time did she abate the din she was making.

'Where's my Ca'line?' he asked eventually, tightening his grip on the woman's arms.

'Your Ca'line,' she screeched, writing with pain, 'she'll not come back to this place!' and she spat in his face.

Jekker released her hair and groped on the table for his knife. Phoebe screamed louder. Overcome by an anger he had never known before, he plunged the blade into her neck until her cries stopped. The woman looked up at him with stricken eyes, then, creeping slowly towards the clothes horse, she pulled down the grey flannel shirt and held it to her throat.

The man stood with one hand pressing on the table top, staring dully at the woman on the floor. The wick in the lamp, which had been unattended for some time, caused a flame to shoot now high, now low, and smoke began to curl above the glass chimney.

'Get up, Phoebe,' said the man. He did not know that he was speaking in a whisper.

The woman muttered something, but her words were not distinguishable. A fold of the grey shirt fell forward softly. It was followed by no other movement. Phoebe could never tell the man now that Caroline's husband was out of gaol, that she had gone back to him. It was a long time before he knew, and then it did not seem to matter much.

SMOKE OF THE TIDE

A fair, middle-aged man with a red face and prominent, light-blue eyes, walked out of the door of a pleasant-looking cottage in the High Street. Dusk was deepening into night as he left, and a few stars showed in the sky directly above him. They looked pale because of a steady red glow that came from the village fair-ground. Over the cottage roofs that stood between him and the fair, strong, black smoke rolled, taking the gleam from the light beneath it. He drew up the smell into his nostrils, and quivered as a certain rapture took hold of him.

The name of the man was Albert Shepherd. He had been born in the cottage which he had just left; indeed, his father and mother still lived there, although all their children had married and left them. Albert was the youngest, and he had been the most successful; that is to say, in northern standards, he had made a lot of brass. He was married to a London woman, and did not often come home, because she could not see the astonishing beauty of the industrial north; she thought it was dirty and depressing. The blue-grey landscapes with their design of mill chimneys – Marion called them smokestacks, and nobody knew what she meant – the rolling hills, the mingling of smoke and cloud, the white steam from the dye-houses, the cobbled streets and houses of blackened stone; all this meant nothing to Marion.

It meant a great deal to Albert Shepherd. He was never fully happy in the south. He loved his wife, and lived there because she liked it best. However, every now and then his homesickness would be too much for him, and he would suddenly say, 'I have to go to Bradford on business.' Each time he asked her to go with him, and each time she refused.

He had not been home in September for years. When he had arrived yesterday there had been a great commotion on the Green. Steam wagons were clanking and snorting, and caravans were springing up like mushrooms across the road from the spare ground. Children were running about shrieking, 'The Tide – the Tide's come!'

It was twenty years since he had smelt the smoke of the Tide. Here, a fair was called either a Feast or a Tide; mostly the latter. He recalled how often he, and the other boys in the school close by, had heard the measured hammering as the Tide was being set up, and how they had longed for the morning to go and the evening to come so that they could rush in and see everything, and spend their money. Even when the money was spent there were other things to watch; other people spending theirs, sometimes winning, more often losing, at games of chance.

This Saturday night, twenty years after, he wanted just as badly to go again. For some whim, he had put only one and sixpence in his pocket. He remembered thinking, when he was ten, that one and sixpence would have been the ideal sum to take to the Tide. When he had had only threepence it had seemed that the very fruits of paradise could have been got for one and six. Well, he would see.

He hastened his footsteps to get there, rattling his coppers in his fingers, and whistling the tune that, out of three, came loudest to his ears through the air.

Raucous shouts, laughter, raised voices, blaring music, the occasional ring of a bell as some champion mallet-slinger touched the tam-o'-shanter of Donald Dinnie, met him as he entered the stall-lined avenue. Here were children's toys, balloons, and brandy snap. Always he had wanted to buy some brandy snap, but his mother would never let him have any. Instead, she made her own, and sometimes, if she left it a second too long in the oven, it was burnt a deep brown, instead of being the pale yellow of his dreams. At last he would have some. As other people were waiting before him he saw the price. 'Nay,' he thought, 'if I spend fourpence of my one and six I shan't have much left.' Casting a lingering glance at the yellow brandy snap, he moved away.

There was so much to see! At one sideshow there were some balls which had merely to be rolled into holes. It looked easy. The amount of the prize was written above each hole, threepence, sixpence – on one, a shilling.

He bought three balls for threepence and rolled them carefully down. The very first one stopped in the shilling place, the second missed, and the third fell into the three-penny hole. He shouted 'Sitha!' as pleased as a child, and instead of trying again he picked up his winnings and walked away, leaving a crowd behind him, gazing and exclaiming after him. He heard a voice saying, 'It's Albert Shepherd, wheer's 'e sprung from?'

He looked about, trying to place the voice, but the seething crowd prevented him from finding out what he wanted to know. Somebody else would be sure to recognise him. He longed wistfully for a friend, one with whom he could share his happiness. He looked up at the hundred waving legs which were rushing through the air not far above him in the Flying Chairs. Each time the machine gyrated, the flying chairs and flying legs came nearer to his head. He wondered whether he dare risk these, and decided not to.

'I'll have six goes on the motor cars with my winnings,' he told himself.

How delightful it was in the motor cars, better by far than in his own. These were upholstered in red plush; they went down a valley, up a hill, down a valley, up a hill with great speed and regularity. He couldn't help saying, 'Whoo-hoo,' each time the motor-car he was in arrived at the exact middle of the dip.

From the centrepiece, inside which a greasy-looking man counted piles of coppers, came the loud, intoxicating blare of a popular song. The second time it was played he hummed it. A little painted image of a man, with a feather in his hat, tapped at a drum, and at each tap a great drum beat from somewhere inside. It was entrancing to meet, on one side, this little iron man, who stared so bravely before him, and tapped away so obediently; yet it was just as entrancing to roll around to the other side, where the real man kept on counting his piles of coppers.

Round and round he went. The faces of all the people in the fairground below were bathed in floods of light. From here he could see little boys darting among the crowd, looking for stray dropped pennies. Albert Shepherd couldn't help laughing to himself. He seemed to be riding above the cares of all the world. There was no time to think of care; always a hill or a valley loomed ahead, and a mad noise urged you on. Away with the dull streets, the hidden offices, the slights and drawbacks even successful men have to meet in business!

Suddenly he thought, 'If only Marion had liked this. If only I had gone to work at the mill every day, like father, and Marion had been happy and contented, like mother. Once a year we could have brought the kids down to the Tide – poor little devils, Marion never lets 'em get within miles of one – and bought 'em a red and yellow wheelbarrow apiece.'

His face clouded over with sadness, to think that they would never know this joy. 'What's in front of them?' he thought; 'the way Marion's bringin' 'em up, they'll soon grow ashamed of her and me.' He made a sudden resolution. He would send for the children in spite of Marion's protests, and let them spend the day with their granny. On Monday night he would take them to the Tide. What did it matter if their bedtime was early, they should stay up until ten for once. Let them get hold of this before their cage claimed them; let them have something bright to look back on. What did it matter if it was tawdry? Everybody needs a bit of tinsel once in a few years.

When he had had four rides, he got up and walked unsteadily down the wooden platform. As he went, he nodded to the little man with the drum.

After the excitement of the cars, it seemed quieter down among the people. Some stopped him and spoke; old men tottering in with their children and grandchildren greeted him and treated him like a boy. 'Nah then, Albert, what's tha' doin' 'ere bi thysel'?'

Over in one corner he met the blacksmith, on whom he had played a number of boyish tricks. He always felt a little ashamed in front of this man. The smith was throwing wooden balls at coconuts, as yet without success. They began to talk together. Some young lads brushed past them, chased by a crowd of shrieking girls with feather dusters in their hands and imitation beetles on the end of tiny wooden ladders.

The blacksmith spat in disgust.

'Lads aren't what they used to be,' he said. 'Now when I wa' smithyin' down at quarry, thirty year sin, lads wor lads. Ther' was one young devil 'at used to play a trick on me ivery morn. 'E used to climb up to t'chimbley, an' put a slate across t'top, an' as sooin as Ah fired up, place filled wi' smoke. Ah niver could remember, an' Ah niver catched 'im, but they don't do things like that now. They daresn't. They run away from lasses i'stead.'

Albert Shepherd looked up at this bulky old man who towered above him and laughed inwardly. It was he who used to climb up and put the slate over the chimney to smoke the blacksmith out, but he did not dare to say so. He bought some wooden balls and began aimlessly throwing them at a young man who was trotting up and down behind a high netting with three hats piled on his head. You had to knock the top one off.

He found he could knock off the hat, or all three hats, quite easily, and did it so many times that the man asked him humbly to stop it. 'I'm not the right chap,' he said, 'and I'm not used to this. The right chap's got a less 'ead than me, and the 'ats fit 'im tighter.'

Excited by his victories, Albert offered to change places with him, and the man came out grinning and rubbing his neck. Soon a crowd drew round, and money poured in. Albert found it hard to walk backwards and forwards in an unconcerned way. As soon as he saw a ball coming, he would flinch and duck, so that his hats were rarely knocked off. He was forced to smile as he wondered what Marion or his business friends would think if they saw him running up and down inside a netting at a fair, having his hat knocked off.

The music from the motor cars, the flying chairs and the roundabouts came all together into his ears. When one tune stopped, and only two strove for mastery, his spirits lowered; as soon as the third tune got up again they returned. All at once, he saw his father and mother. He laughed, and turned away his face, but to no purpose. Through all the din his mother's voice broke accusingly, 'Our Albert, come out!' and he obeyed it, as he had obeyed it a hundred times before, in his younger days.

He went with them to the sideshows, the dartboard and the ringboard; many a game he won. He got boxes of toffee, and eggcups, and china mugs, and strange little ornaments, the kind his mother loved to put on her bedroom mantelpiece. He did not remember when he had last felt so happy.

Each year his mother and father came down to the Tide, just for a walk round, to see old friends; very soon they went back home. This night their son did not go with them. It grew later and later and, one by one, the stalls were shut down. For the last time the harsh music crashed out, and above it you could hear the steady thump, thump of the Tide's heart – the great power engine which drove the roundabouts.

Instead of going home, Albert Shepherd went for a short walk, up a green lane on the hillside. In his pockets a number of pennies still rattled – so far as he had counted he had elevenpence left – and in his nostrils the smell of the thick smoke lingered.

He met a policeman, walking with slow, even steps.

'Good night,' he said; he could see it was Willie Ambler, a boy who had been at school with him.

'Hello, Albert,' said the policeman, 'how long are you over for? Did you come just for t'feeast, like?'

'Ay,' answered Albert, 'I've just had a look in at t'Tide.' Marion hated to hear him talk like this, he reflected.

'It gets worse ivery year, doesn't it?' said the policeman, gazing yearningly over at the spot where the smoke still rolled up to the exquisite midnight sky, in which a full round moon was now sailing.

'Ay,' said Albert. It would never do for them both to confess how deeply they loved it; so they stood there for a long time, until the glow died away, and only the moon was left serenely looking down.

BROTHER W

A man of about sixty sat in a crowded railway carriage thinking so deeply that he might have been alone. Though the night was wet and the air raw, perspiration formed in the thin hair at his temples, and made a frustrated effort to run down his cheeks. He wore a bowler hat, a high, dirtyish-white collar, under which was an imitation shirt-front of purple paper made up by himself, and a new black overcoat, too large for him.

Owing to some malformation, he could never quite shut his right eye, the under lid of which, bright red and shining, seemed to be pinned down on to his cheek. His eyes were large, a pale greenish-grey. He had a grey moustache. As he sat, his hands, coming out of their long sleeves, clasped loosely on his knees, his expression was one of extreme misery.

The carriage of the local train was badly lighted. It had a low, yellowish-white roof, smeared and dirty. The seats were of horsehair, smooth, slippery, and cold. On the uneven floor were several small pools, made by the rain from umbrellas, which trickled for a time like springs. Sleet, falling sideways on the steamed windows, ran a straight, heavy course to the window-bottoms; in one case entering the carriage and running down the horsehair at every jolt. Workmen smoked and jested. Two or three young girls, laughing and breathless from their last-minute jump on to the train, compared notes interminably. 'I thought we were never going to catch it' – 'I've torn my stocking, what a nuisance' – 'Look at Hilda, hasn't she got a red face?' – 'You look at your own!' – 'Didn't we have to run for it?'

All the time the elderly man, William Aykroyd, stared in front of him, blinking rapidly, as he always did, to keep his right eye clear. He did not want to go home, only habit was driving him back. He was a bachelor. His brother James, also a bachelor, with whom he had always lived, had died just a week ago. He began to think about his brother – 'young' James – three years his junior. Their father had died fifty, their mother thirty, years ago. They had lived, the two of them, together for almost thirty years, and for twenty of them, he, William, had not spoken to his brother James.

He remembered the trivial quarrel which had started his long silence. It had seemed such a big thing at the time. James had slyly borrowed his new suit, and gone out in it without permission, and William could not forgive him. William did not say a word when the culprit returned, he merely ignored him, did not listen to his explanations, and refused to speak to him. For twenty years he had kept this up. At first James, round-faced, merry-eyed, improvident James, had taken it as a huge joke, teasing him, taking his arm and walking with him to the train, calling him 'Brother W.,' pretending it was more formal than 'William,' and in other ways trying to break down the ridiculous barrier which pride had raised between them.

William refused to respond. Both he and his brother worked as compositors for a jobbing printer. They had worked together, but after a year or two James made a change, so that he should not be continually near his silent brother. At that time, if William were compelled to send word about work to James, he would always do it through a third person. He would call up a boy and say, 'Go, tell James Aykroyd that William Aykroyd wants him to do so-and-so.' Early on, James would send exaggerated messages back, to which William pretended not to listen.

The brothers took their lunches and ate them in front of the rusty iron stove at the bottom end of the room. During the lunch hour the gas engine which ran the clanking machinery stopped. The smell of ink and lye pervaded the room. Sometimes they were alone, as the other men and the machine-feeders went home on fine days, and for an hour there would be no sound but the chink of a cinder as it fell out of the stove, or the rustle of the paper in which their food was wrapped. Neither of them went out for fresh air. They would read old newspapers, or James would borrow a 'blood' from one of the boys. If they did not read they would look at the stove or out of the grimy windows.

James could never get used to the silence. He kept forgetting, and saying something excitedly to his brother: 'Tip's coming to the Hippodrome next week!' or, 'What do you think of City's chances for the Cup, now?' after a win at football. William's mouth would tighten, he would look away, and after a minute James would get up with a crestfallen look, and he would take a turn around the room.

James was always trying to break the silence. Both brothers frequented the one music hall of the town. James, hiding his round face behind his coat collar, would stand near to his brother in the queue, and as they entered would endeavour to sit beside him. When they were both laughing at some joke, James would turn and say, 'Wasn't that a good one?' but he had never caught his brother off guard. As soon as there was an interval, William would rise and change his seat, even choosing a worse place.

At home, their life became strange, almost unbelievable. There were only two bedrooms in the house. The boys had grown up together, and had always slept in the same bed. After the death of their mother, neither of them showed any desire to move, to have a separate room. They continued sleeping together, even after the quarrel, in the same rickety iron bed they had always slept in. When they got up the first thing they did was to throw back the bedclothes. Before leaving for work they would turn the mattress and make the bed, ready for night.

Each made his own breakfast. Each had a gas ring and a small pan. They made tea and boiled an egg or fried a little bacon separately. They cut from separate loaves of home-made bread. On Wednesday evening of one week James would come home, light a fire, set the oven on, and bake a sufficient quantity of bread to last the two of them a week. The next Wednesday would be William's turn. Their mother had taught them to bake; they would never have dreamed of buying their bread. All other food they bought separately, each getting what he needed.

James began to lose his spirits after a year or two of silence on his brother's part. Sometimes he would say humbly, 'The bread's very nice this week, William,' hoping for some reply, but none ever came.

The train was drawing near the station. One of the young girls rubbed the dirty window with the back of her glove, but instead of looking out merely showed the soiled glove to her companions with a look of exasperation. A workman knocked his pipe against the iron-rimmed sole of his boot. William Aykroyd stood up and took from the rack an old leather bag to which the smell of stale bread clung. He sat forward on the seat, holding his bag with both hands, looking as if he were almost anxious to be out of the train and away to some warm, comfortable home in which he would be enveloped with loving care.

Ten minutes later he opened the door of his house. His new coat glistened with melting snow and raindrops. He felt in his pocket for matches, lit the gas, and pulled down the paper blind. It was Wednesday, time for the bread to be baked. He lit the fire with waiting coal and chips, and drew out the oven damper. Running some water, he put the pan on the gas-ring, but forgot to light it. He had intended to make some tea. Lately he had often forgotten. There seemed to be no use making tea when James was not there to irritate him. James was extravagant, he had saved very little money, and would often bring good things home for his tea; a piece of fish or meat to fry, and some vanillas, of which he was very fond, for what he called a 'finisher-off.' William, more frugal, contented himself with a sausage, a small meat pie, or another egg.

As soon as the fire began to make itself felt, William washed his hands and set the baking bowl to warm in front of the blaze. He emptied a packet of flour into the bowl, and rubbed lard and salt into it. He lit the gas ring under the neglected pan of water, and took from a shelf a small packet of yeast. When the dough was kneaded and rising he sat on a low stool in front of the fire, so near that steam arose from his damp trouser legs. The house was silent, except for the drone made by a strong flame driven under the oven damper.

After he had sat for a few minutes he got up and opened a cupboard door, taking from the top shelf a large jug full of silver coins, all the money that his brother James had saved during his fifty-six years of life. There would be no more than thirty pounds, William knew. He had counted it before. He had decided, coming home in the train, to use the money to buy a tombstone for his brother.

Even as he so resolved he could not believe that his brother was dead. James had been brought home a fortnight ago, unconscious, and had lain in bed for a week. William had gone out immediately to fetch a doctor, and a woman, a neighbour, who knew something about nursing, to look after his brother. Just before the end – on the Tuesday night – the neighbour, Mrs Pigott, came running downstairs shouting nervously, 'He's conscious, Mr Aykroyd!'

William remembered how he had gone up the stairs into the cold bedroom, with its inadequate gas flare, and seen

James lying helpless in bed, moving his stiff lips, saying, 'Will'am,' with great difficulty, over and over again. And William had stood looking at him, with water – perhaps tears – running out of his never-shut eye, struggling to answer, 'I am here, James,' but some demon had pressed a hand over his mouth. It was no use; after not speaking to his brother for twenty years he could not do it now. Then James's voice had become silent, the flickering light had faded from his eyes; he was dead.

As he cut up the dough and put it into the blackened loaf-tins, William thought about the funeral, about himself and the thin young parson riding in the solitary cab, about the three wreaths of flowers, one from himself, one from the neighbours, and one from James's workmates. He thought about the new grave that he had bought because the family grave would hold no more, and of the extra money he had given to have it bricked. He had paid for everything, not knowing that James had saved thirty pounds. Now there should be a splendid tombstone for him.

Just as he had never wished to sleep in the other bedroom after his mother had died, now he did not wish to sleep upstairs at all. He had brought bedding down and made a bed on the old couch, and it pleased him. He shut off the upper part of the house, pretending it was not there. He liked to go to bed in the firelight, in a strange room, so that he would not feel so lonely or miss James so greatly. He felt that he would like to call out, 'James, are you there?' but even yet, he could not do it.

The bread was baked at last, its warm smell filled the little living room. It was late enough to go to bed. William took off his clothes, tearing the paper front as he did so. This was an idea of his own, to save washing. He had a fresh one every day, as he could get the paper for nothing. He remembered how James used to laugh at these different-coloured fronts, which were sometimes blue, sometimes green, or as today, purple. He used to laugh at the purple ones. Just before he got into bed, William opened his leather bag and was astonished to find that his lunch was still there. He must have forgotten to eat it. He thought it would do for the next day. He shut his eyes, but his mind stayed awake, thinking of James.

The next day, at lunchtime, he rolled up his apron and put on his long black coat. It was fine, but very cold. He had noticed a sign, near the cemetery, 'Roland Tonks, Monumental Mason.' He thought he would go to see Roland Tonks, whose name pleased him.

The shop which he entered was filled with fancy stones and marbles. There was also a yard, in which a man was working, but this held only small crosses and stone slabs, some with unfinished inscriptions on them. As he waited for Mr Tonks, who presently came in exhaling an odour of mutton and onions, William read through a glass window the bald, sad names – Agnes Wetherall, John George White, Roger Suddards – which advertised to casual passers-by that still another body was gone to crumble in the forgetting earth.

Mr Tonks seemed to have the idea that William was married, and that it was his wife who had died; and was continually suggesting, with his head on one side, that he thought something with a nice female figure – 'an angel, perhaps?' – would do for 'her.'

In the corner of the room stood a granite obelisk, eight or nine feet high. William kept looking at it. It seemed remote, a thing apart from the rolls and scrolls. It reminded him of his twenty years' silence to James. All the time that Mr Tonks talked to him he looked at the great stone.

'How much will this one be?' he asked at length, putting out his hand and touching the cold, glittering granite.

'That's something rather better. That is, indeed, a monument,' answered Mr Tonks; 'but perhaps it's a little dear, a little more than you might like to give. It's a hundred pounds.'

Many days after this, William came again to look at the obelisk. He had not yet made a decision and Mr Tonks was getting disheartened. People often came to his shop in great grief, and if he could not help them to decide, sometimes they said they would 'leave it till later,' and when they had given it a little more thought, left it for ever.

He was surprised when William came one Saturday to order the granite monument.

'You see,' explained his customer slowly, 'There's two brothers. I'd like you to write, "In memory of James Aykroyd," then he pulled a small notebook from his pocket, and gave the dates of his brother's birth and death.

'After that, put, "Also of his brother William, born –"' When he had given the date, he hung back, perplexed.

'You'll have to wait,' he said; 'I can't give you the date of William's death.'

'If you send me a note, it'll do,' said Mr Tonks comfortingly. He was at his desk, writing out a receipt, and casting covert, happy looks at the wad of notes William had brought.

William's face was drawn and thin. His pale eyes, the right one seeming to bulge out over its reddened lid, looked as if they had been sleepless for a long time. His movements were uncertain, and he listened to the voice of the other man with strained attention.

'I'll send you a note when I get home,' he said; 'that is, when I've had time to look it up. Have you got it written down, "Also of his brother William?"'

'Yes,' said Mr Tonks. 'And we'll see that only the very best work is put into it. You wouldn't like a verse, perhaps?' he suggested.

'No,' answered William. 'Good day.'

'You're forgetting your receipt, Mr Aykroyd,' called Mr Tonks, trying to speak sadly, and not succeeding.

Early the following week, Mr Tonks received a note, written simply on a soiled envelope. It was delivered by hand, and read, 'Brother W. Died – ' Here followed a date, written clearly.

'Why,' said Mr Tonks, examining in perplexity first the note and then the calendar hanging near his head, 'that's today.'

ACCIDENT

A woman was sitting in a café about eleven o'clock one morning, taking sips from a cup of weak tea and eating a cream bun, without knowing she was doing so. She had a bad headache.

On the chair by her side – there were four chairs altogether around the table – she had placed a pair of thin brown gloves and a handbag. She kept looking at these from time to time. They were smeared with drying blood, as was the front of her dress; and each time she looked at them she groaned audibly.

Two waitresses, not yet in their uniforms, still occupied with cleaning out the café, ready for the lunch hour rush, kept peering at her from the door of the kitchen. Every now and then the cook joined them, and they all cast puzzled glances at their solitary customer, eating and drinking like an automaton.

The name of this woman was Mrs Leveritt. She was between forty and forty-five years of age, and had brown eyes and a clear skin. Normally, she would have colour, but just now her face was drawn and pale. She did not seem to notice the waitresses or the cook, but was utterly possessed with one inward thought, to the exclusion of anything else.

She had a husband and three children. Not having married until she was almost thirty, her children were still quite young – indeed, they were all at school. Her husband was a joiner. She had married him because he had come after her for several years, and she liked him.

When she was young, she had been full of romance, a very high-handed girl. She wasn't going to marry anybody just for the sake of getting married. She was going to wait until somebody came with whom she could fall in love. She knew exactly how it would happen; she would see him, know him in a moment. This would be the man for whom she would leave father, mother, and home. There would be no mistake; they would both know.

But first her mother died, then her father. Fred Leveritt, who came to the house every Wednesday and Saturday – pretending to come for her father's sake, but really, she knew, to see her – had told her that the best thing she could do was to marry him. She was very fond of Fred, he was most kind, and he thought the world about her. So she had married Fred.

How calm and happy her life had been with him. She looked no older than when she was married. Her three children had suffered only from minor ailments, except Phyllis, the eldest, who had once had to go to hospital with fever. Their home was comfortable. Fred had made a great deal of the furniture, and she kept it polished bright and shining. Every year, for one week, they went to the seaside with the children, and had a good time, whether the weather was wet or fine.

This morning she had set off, soon after getting the children to school, to do some ordinary shopping. She wanted to make a steak and kidney pie for dinner. Just as she got to the crossroads she saw there was an accident.

She had been looking into a shop window as she walked on and did not actually see the accident happen. But there was a lorry, and a boy with a sick white face climbing out of the driver's seat; and, on the ground, some yards away, a man was lying.

Mrs Leveritt's first impulse was to run away. Indeed, her feet actually turned, and when she came to her normal, kindly senses, she was going rather rapidly in another direction. With just such another whirl, she turned; and she was the one on whose knee the injured man's head was pillowed, and hers was the face on which he looked as he opened his eyes.

What happened next, Mrs Leveritt was not sure. There must have been a crowd of people, and the boy coming limping up out of the lorry, and a policeman somewhere. There must have been somebody ringing up in the nearby telephone box for an ambulance, because soon one came.

But for Mrs Leveritt, and the man whose head she held in her arms, there was a moment of complete understanding. It was as if the world had stopped around them, and they were enclosed in a lovely crystal ball, looking for ever into each other's eyes, made perfect by love.

The crystal ball burst with a crash. Before she could draw her thoughts again into focus, everything had disappeared;

the man, the ambulance, the policeman, the crowd. She had not seen the accident happen, therefore she was of no use as a witness. She walked a long way before, at last, she entered the café and ordered tea. The waitress put some stale cakes near her, and she ate mechanically.

At last she had to go home. Realising that there was no time to make the pie, she hastily prepared a plainer dinner for the children, looked after their needs, and sent them off to school again.

In the evening, after her husband had come home and had his meal, a knock came at the door. She was washing up. Hastily drying her hands on her apron she ran to open the door. She was expecting a message. She knew not what, nor when it would come; but that it would reach her she was certain.

However, it was only Ted Rhodes, a friend of Fred's. Ted was also a joiner, but he was mostly on outside work, and was often a little stiff with rheumatism. The two men smoked and talked, and, for some reason, as soon as her work was done, the woman sat and listened to every word attentively. At the same time the other half of her brain was wondering when she could go to the hospital to visit the injured man, and if they would let her see him.

Suddenly Ted said, 'A mate o' mine was run over with a lorry this morning and killed. Kitson 'is name was. Lived over other side o' Shawford, near brickworks.'

Fred didn't know him.

Mrs Leveritt gave a great sigh. Here was the message.

'What was he like?' she asked, twisting her lips into a solemn smile.

'Like? Let me see,' said Ted. He thought for a minute. 'A tall chap, wi' greyish 'air and plenty o' colour. D'you know 'im?'

'I think so,' she answered, very quietly.

A tall chap, with greyish hair and plenty of colour. That was all she had to remember. And he had gone out into the dark, taking her love with him.

THE END OF THE QUEUE

A boy of fourteen jumped out of bed as soon as he heard his mother's voice calling 'Jonty' from the bottom of the attic stairs. The bed was opposite the dormer window, through which only an expanse of dull grey sky was to be seen. He shouted 'I'm coming,' in a voice so loud that his younger brother, who slept in the same bed, woke with a convulsive start and sat suddenly upright, his eyes and mouth opened wide in surprise and fear. Jont took no notice of the little boy, but after placing a red wooden chair under the window, climbed on to it and put his face through the small square that was open.

He could see some shining grey roofs, a hen house in a field, a length of iron railing, and two or three pools in the road beneath him. 'It's raining,' he said, in a very quiet, disappointed way.

'Oh,' answered his brother, who had been sitting up in the same dazed manner since the noise had first awakened him; and he lay down again immediately, put his knees up to his chin, and was asleep in a minute.

The elder boy, whose name was Jonathan, but who was never called anything but Jont or Jonty, got dressed in the

41

clothes which he had put ready for himself very neatly. This morning was the beginning of a new life for him. He had left school, and was now going to help his father in what was known as 'the business'. He had been dreaming during the night of colossal tasks that had been set for him, over which he was taking more time than was humanly possible. And he was glad to wake up, to jump out of bed, and to look quickly through the window.

There seemed to be a fresh meaning in life. The very sound of his feet padding down the creaking attic stairs was different. He could not wait for the water in the tap to run warm, but washed himself in cold, so impatient was he to be off to work.

Downstairs, his father was already bent over a basin of porridge and treacle, the drooping points of his grey moustache dark with moisture. The boy had a great respect for his father, and felt proud when he thought that every day, now, he would walk at his side into town, up the steps where 'the business' was, into the dim little office, and be a sort of prince under his father, the king.

At school, he used to boast of 'our place', because there were so many boys whose fathers just went out to work for wages. There was something romantic in being able to take boys into the warehouse, to sniff up the pervading smell of leather, to point out the long rows of shoe boxes with their bronze labels showing Daisy or Beeko or Candid brands; and to steal quietly up to the far end, where there was the tiny gas-lit office with the glass window opening into the warehouse, near which his father usually sat.

For some reason unknown to the boy, his mother had been crying, and she moved about in silence, stopping every now and then to rock with her foot an old-fashioned brown wooden cradle in which a very small, delicate baby was lying.

'How's Ronald?' he asked in a whisper, pulling out a chair and sitting down on it.

'Put your boots on, do,' answered his mother. 'How many times must I tell you not to walk about the bare oilcloth in your stockings? Ronald's had a very poor night.'

'Oh,' he said, in imitation of his father's manner, 'dear me.' And he began eating his breakfast, looking out of the windows and watching the thin rain dropping into the shallow pools on the path, or following the course of a leaf falling from one of the higher trees. There were many wet, yellow leaves already lying about. At the same time, without haste, he pushed his feet into his boots which were under the table.

The new life did not seem to be beginning very well. There was not much difference here from any other day. He might have been getting ready for school, for all his mother seemed to care. She went about in an unsmiling way, preparing food for the delicate baby. Even the fire was dull and comfortless. The coal caked together, black and sulky, only opening here and there to show a meagre streak of red.

So the boy ate, and imagined himself grown up, say eighteen or nineteen. The boxes on the warehouse shelves gleamed and shone. The little office was transformed. There was even electric light and a radiator in it, and bright new ledgers in green and red bindings. He saw himself sitting in a swivel chair, whizzing first one way and then the other. A young boy was calling him 'Sir.' He smiled secretly.

His mother came out of the door at the cellar-head, carrying a shovel with a small quantity of coal on it.

'We shall have to get some more coal,' she said, looking across at her husband. 'You'd better call at Scott's on your way down.'

Her husband turned and looked at her, but he only said 'Hannah!' quietly.

'I don't care.' She raised her voice and then looked towards the cradle. 'We shall have to get some more,' she repeated stubbornly.

The father and son set off as soon as they were ready, Jonty walking under a large umbrella with a yellow handle which his father held up. Some of their neighbours were already setting off. They looked with smiling surprise at the boy under the umbrella, who was short for his years. He wore a school cap over his fair hair, and his knees showed mottled between the tops of his socks and his short trousers. He was walking carefully, avoiding the puddles as well as he could, trying all at once to become grown up and to behave as his father did. He even assumed the distant, yet worried expression that was on his father's face.

As they passed one house, a big, black-haired boy with a heavy jowl came to the window, pulled a face, and surreptitiously shook his fist at the pair. Jont flinched, and shrank a little closer to his father's side, putting out his hand so that it touched a damp pocket flap. But after a second he moved away, turned round, and stuck out his tongue at the jowled lad, as a gesture of defiance. 'After all,' he thought, 'I go to work now. I'm not a kid any longer.' And it seemed to him that he was already a man, past being bullied in any way whatsoever.

The warehouse felt cold. There was nothing for him to do after he had lit the stove and swept up the dirty floor. He wanted very much to tidy all the boxes, straighten the shoes, rearrange the two flaps of white paper in each box, even to put a pair of laces to match in every one. But his father would not let him do this.

He kept looking about him, brightly at first, then more and more dully. It was a great treat to him when he found a calendar that was many months behindhand. He brought it up to date, tearing off each day separately and carefully, and putting the papers in a heap on the floor, ready to be taken away.

His father had taken off his outdoor coat, and put on a very old, shabby office coat, the lining of which showed at the elbows; and now sat in his sloping chair, looking at the stove. Sometimes he put a hand on the desk, and drew papers towards himself in a hesitating way; then he pushed them back, as if he were not certain what to do with them. After a while, he roused himself.

'Would you like to run an errand, Jont?' he muttered, so low that his son scarcely heard him.

'Yes,' said the boy, jumping up joyfully as soon as the meaning of the words came to him. He felt that he had been shut in the office for many hours, though in reality it was not much past ten o'clock.

'Take the umbrella, if it's still raining,' said his father, now definitely drawing some papers towards himself, and writing a note very quickly.

'Oh, *no*, father,' said Jont, putting on his cap and his short, shabby raincoat, 'it'll have stopped raining by now. I won't need the umbrella.'

His father was not listening, but was busy putting his note into an envelope and licking down the flap.

The boy's spirits rose at the thought of getting outside, of seeing the interesting sights in the streets, of once more being among people. He seemed to have been shut in some forgotten tomb with his father for a long time.

As he went down the steps into the street, closing the clumsy-looking wooden door carefully behind him, he almost bumped into a sharp-featured boy of his own age, dressed in a suit of very shiny serge and carrying a large parcel.

'Hello,' said the boy, 'are you t'new lad 'ere?'

'Ye-es,' said Jont, looking at him without smiling. 'Why?'

'Nay, I only wanted to knaw. I knew t'last lad.' They fell into step. 'You've got a funny cove for t'boss,' he went on. 'Puts Wholesale on 'is door, and sells boots retail to anybody 'at comes in t'back way for 'em.'

Jont thought over this. 'How do you know?' he asked with curiosity.

''Ow do I knaw? Because I've 'ad some,' answered the lad. 'These is a pair.' He kicked up his right foot, almost overbalancing as he did so.

Jont walked on at his side, wondering whether to offer to

help the lad with his parcel. He said in a mild voice, 'It's my father.'

'Aw,' said the other. They walked on for a while without speaking. 'Which way are you going?' he asked at last.

Jont found that he did not want to tell the lad his destination. At random, he said, 'Canal Road.'

'If I 'adn't this parcel, I'd come wi' you.'

Jont was glad because of the parcel. At a corner they parted without saying goodbye. The boy called after him, 'What's your name?'

'My name's Jonathan Gresham. What's yours?'

'Mind yer own business,' said the lad rudely. And for some time afterwards, Jont was tormented every time he put his head outside the door by the words 'My name is Jonathan Gresham,' repeated in a mincing voice by some person in hiding.

He went on with a dragging step, pondering over the answer he ought to have returned to the sharp-faced boy. The rain was still falling finely on to his face. He began to think of an invention, an umbrella which should be clamped on the head, with an upturned rim from which the rainwater would pour every time you bowed.

He half-pulled the letter from his pocket to look once more at the address. On the back, in his father's handwriting, were the words, Mr Goldstone, Gower Buildings, Maud Street. He knew that Maud Street was a short thoroughfare between two of the main squares of the town, where there were grim, high buildings filled with small offices.

The office of Mr Goldstone was on the very top floor. The boy climbed up a spiral stone staircase, listening to the noisy echo, 'shisha, shish' made by his feet. Behind doors fitted with ground glass panels, he saw figures moving like black shadows, or heard the sound of a quick-driven typewriter. Occasionally a voice or a laugh cut into the silence.

As he neared the top, the stairway narrowed. He raised his eyes, and saw above him a queue of people waiting; some holding the banister rail, some leaning against the wall; all sinister and quiet, watching his approach with dull eyes. There was something hopeless about their lounging figures. The boy's small, erect shape, his school cap, even his bare knees seemed to interest them in a morbid way. They were all waiting outside the last door, on which was written in thick black letters, 'I Goldstone, Money on Loan.'

The boy, in his turn, stared at them with large, innocent eyes. Each one had a red book in his hand, and one or two were clinking coins together, very quietly. He wished that his father had not sent him to this place. What connection could there be between his father and a moneylender? Was he taking a receipt for some shoes that Mr Goldstone had bought retail?

He made his way steadily forward, through the queue of people, saying 'Please,' in a gentle voice, or 'Excuse me.' Some made way for him willingly, some apathetically, but all in silence. He opened the door at the top. Inside was a small cubicle, where a man in a thin grey coat and bowler hat was leaning forward, writing figures with a short pencil on a piece of brown paper. Behind the small counter a dark, fat man was sitting at a low desk. This man looked up with a frown as the door opened.

'What do you want?' he said, in an unpleasant voice.

The boy was frightened, and because of his fear his heart began to beat quickly, and he felt short of breath.

'Please,' he said, 'I've brought a letter from Gresham & Co.'

'Oh,' said the man, staring at him, 'go wait at the end of the queue.'

The boy did not seem to understand him. 'I've brought this from my father,' he said, struggling to get the envelope out of his pocket. 'Mr Gresham's sent me from the office.' He wished the dark man to know he was business-like.

'Is that so?' said the dark man, his voice still more unpleasant. 'Do as I tell you. Go stand at the end of the queue. Take your turn.' And all the time the man in the thin coat went on writing with his stumpy pencil.

The boy felt behind him for the door knob with his free hand. His eyes became covered with a film. He felt as if somebody was strangling him, pressing a thumb on his throat, just where he was wanting to swallow. He wished that he could be struck dead so that he would not have to move any more.

Slowly he pulled open the door, went down a few steps, and stood, his head bowed, his back to the others, looking through a small staircase window at the rain-wet wall opposite, trying not to think about the envelope in his hand, which he now knew contained no receipt, no money, but only some kind of an excuse.

After he had stood for a while, he lifted his head and began to whistle, at first hesitatingly, but then with more confidence, a song he had learned at school; the sound that came from his lips was quiet, but as pure as a bird's song.

49

'Twas on the morn of sweet Mayday
When nature painted all things gay,
Taught birds to sing and lambs to play . . .

And presently it seemed that a ripple of hope passed through the waiting company, and took away a little of the heaviness from it. Nobody told him to be quiet, so the boy went on whistling his tune, moving upward step by step.

THE LONELY ONE

A mother was giving last instructions to her daughter before going out into the howling wind of a grey winter's day.

'Remember, Aunt Annie'll be here in an hour, but if she shouldn't turn up till dinner time, be careful of everything. Tell 'er the soup's ready in the oven, it's thickened, and the 'taties are in and all. There'll be nought for 'er to do beyond wash up, and you can 'elp 'er. Now be a good lass, and heed your auntie. You can fetch the milk at a quarter to five, and I s'll be back as soon as I can get away. Ee dear, I wish I 'adn't to go.'

The mother stood in front of a small, cork-framed mirror, pursing her lips and lifting her chin as she wrapped a long black scarf two or three times round her neck before tying it. She had put on a couple of coats and a shawl, and two extra flannel skirts, as well as two pairs of stockings and some galoshes. She was going to a funeral – that of her late husband's sister, at Oxenthorp – and had made up her mind that she would keep herself warm. She was not yet forty, but she was quite convinced that one funeral made many, and did not want to be the next victim of that mysterious and inexorable thing, death.

Her expression was worried and preoccupied, as she had an arduous journey before her. She finished tying the scarf, and said, 'There now, I think that's all. Pass my umbrella, Margaret Ann.'

She felt hastily in her pocket to see that her purse was still safe, and moved her chin above the unaccustomed, crepe-smelling scarf. Now that she was quite ready, her mind filled with all the things she had been going to do. She was breathing loudly and nervously, and looking round the kitchen with bright, quick-moving eyes. How hateful it was to leave home, to go to Oxenthorp, to think of the sadness, the eating, the washing-up, the coming conversation about the dead Sarah.

'Don't break the teapot,' she said in rather an angry voice.

The child looked at her in astonishment, then said breathlessly, 'If you don't go, mother, you'll miss the bus.' It seemed as if the bubble of the moment had held together too long, and that something must break it.

The mother opened the inner door, and stepped out into the stone porch. The cold was bitter, and wind swept in through the cracks. The little girl shivered and backed into the warmth of the kitchen. When the outer door was opened, a cutting blast blew in, rushed about, and took the heated air with it up the chimney. The path rang hard as iron beneath her mother's feet. She gave a loud shudder as she pushed the door shut, and blew on her chilled hands. Then she ran to the window, and waved until her mother was out of sight.

Snow began to fall, not in soft, patterned particles that clung to the window-pane, but in sharp, stinging fragments that hissed down the wind, and made the bitter day more bitter yet. The sky was leaden and low; every living thing was out of sight.

The child was alone in the cottage, except for a small, half-grown black cat. She felt proud and important, being left in charge even for an hour. She sat on a low chair in front of the fire, talking to the cat, which she had picked up and seated forcibly on her knee.

'Pussy Allison,' she said in a loud, gruff voice, 'this is *my* house, and *I'm* your mother now!'

The cat twisted its head, clawed at her cloth frock, and then made the sound 'wew' in a tiny, resigned voice.

'Let's go look for auntie,' she said in her own clear, childish tones. She lifted up the cat and made it look through the window for a long time. It was freezingly cold there, and the cat kept trying to get back to the warmth of the fire. There was no sign of auntie, and the snow was blowing faster, almost blotting out the two melancholy, leafless willow trees at the bottom of the garden.

The little girl began to feel sad. The breakfast things were still lying on the table, her mother's blue and white cup and saucer, and her own pink mug. There was a jar of jam with a frilled paper hanging from it, on which was written, 'Rasp. and Goose, July 15.' Although she was full, she could not resist dipping a teaspoon once in the jam jar and licking off the half-sweet, half-sour stuff.

The grandfather clock, which stood in a corner with its head and foot sawn off – the room was very low – suddenly gave a loud whirr and struck three times. It was ten o'clock. Margaret Ann started and gulped, and her glance went involuntarily to a flowered text hanging a little crookedly above the mantelshelf.

She thought she would do some work as a surprise for her aunt. After pushing the things to the back of the table, she fetched an enamel bowl from the scullery sink. Oh, it was cold in the scullery! Even the stone floor was slippery, and ice stood on the top of the bucket of drinking water.

There was hot water in a boiler by the fireside. She lifted up the lid, and carried some in a tin lading-can to her bowl. Then she stood up on a three-legged stool and slowly washed the breakfast things. Her hands immediately became red, and swelled. Each time she lifted them out of the water they itched and hurt. She was glad to dry them, glad when the things were done and put away. It was no use emptying the water down the sink, as the outlet pipe was frozen; so she left it in the bowl.

What could she do? She mended the fire and played with the cat, reading aloud to it from a picture book. Every few minutes she went to look out of the window, but there was nothing to be seen beyond the grey, wind-lashed willows and the powder-like snow, which was already drifting against the wall of the coalhouse, though the space immediately in front of the cottage was clear. It seemed to the child that as soon as her aunt arrived, everything would be different, and the time would pass quickly and happily.

At twelve o'clock she was still alone, so the little girl got a basin from the cupboard, and carefully opening the oven door, ladled out some soup for herself and some for the cat. They sat at opposite sides of the hearth, lapping daintily. The child kept stopping to hum a tune, and to wonder what she could do all afternoon if her aunt did not come.

She wished that they had a neighbour. Although there were two cottages standing together, one of them was at the moment empty. How good it would be to talk to somebody, just for five minutes! She sighed.

When her soup was eaten, she took her basin and spoon and the cat's saucer into the scullery. No good making a washing up for that. She wished that the snow would pile high in front of the door, so that she could shovel it away. But instead of doing so, the snow blew away from the doorspace, as though it intended to keep one place bleak and bare. She remembered that she had promised her mother not to go outside except for the milk; and wondered if the whole world would be snowed up at a quarter to five.

She went upstairs, and pretended to make the bed. But she only straightened it, without turning the flock mattress over. She knew that her mother would re-make it, yet she might perhaps be glad that Margaret Ann had tried. The bed felt both cold and damp. Was it possible that she would be sleeping beside her mother tonight, all snug and warm, except for the tip of her nose? The night before, it had been so chilly that when she stretched out her hand her mother's hair had felt as cold as a dead bird's feathers.

In the bedroom she began to jump about and sing sadly but defiantly, 'Snow, snow faster, white allyblaster, killing geese in Scotland, sending feathers here.' She jumped more quickly, and even turned a somersault over the bed before looking out of the window again.

Somebody was struggling along the road – a woman, with an umbrella behind her back. Surely it was her aunt at last. For some seconds there was a lull in the storm, and the figure strode along a little faster. Why didn't she wave? Margaret Ann thought perhaps she had got some snow down her neck; she looked as stiff as a bobbing doll.

The little girl ran downstairs, ready to open the door. She stood behind it, excited and happy. Should she hide, and make Aunt Annie look for her, or should she jump out and say 'Boo!' No, she would be a good little girl, and say, 'Good afternoon, auntie, have you had your dinner?'

But nobody came. The woman must have been a stranger, or somebody from the next village. As soon as she realised that nothing fresh was to happen, that the woman had passed, the child sat down in front of the fire and cried a little, pouting her lips and narrowing her eyes, but very few tears came. Her mother was far away and her auntie had forgotten her. Forgotten her! Yes, that was better. One real tear fell down her left cheek, and another stood in the corner of her right eye.

Darkness drew in early, and with it came a cold still more intense. It was difficult, almost impossible, to keep warm. All the heat from the fire seemed to go up the chimney, instead of coming out into the room. If you sat so near that smoke went up from your dress front, your elbows and your back were frozen.

The little girl kept watching the clock, counting the seconds as they were ticked out. When it became really dark, she lit the lamp and sat down again to read fairy tales to the cat, holding it tight so that she could keep her hands warm. The cat was angry and uncomfortable, and sprang away as soon as it could, so she put her hands under her armpits, and kept on reading aloud in a flat, metallic voice from *The Tinder Box*.

Soon after four o'clock she made herself ready to go for the milk. Here was a change. She got her cap and coat and scarf, her woollen gloves and her gaiters. She wondered whether to take the cat beneath her coat, but the cat seemed to divine her intention, and hid itself out of sight. Then she got the shiny brown milk jug with the lid over it, and sat waiting until it was time to go. There was no sense in blowing out the light or locking the door; nobody would come near on a night like this.

Fine snow had drifted into the porch at last; the child made a footprint in it before she opened the door. She had difficulty in shutting the heavy door, and as she struggled with it, the bitter wind blew into her ears.

She set off bravely down the road towards the farm, and as she walked she thought about the farmer, Mr Jepson. He was a man who lived quite alone, rarely speaking to anybody except the dairyman who came morning and evening to collect the milk. The little girl wanted to talk to somebody, as she had been silent so long, and she thought of all the things she would say to Mr Jepson. She would tell him about Aunt Annie not coming. He liked to hear her talk about Aunt Annie. He would answer, 'Is she, now?' or 'Does she, now?' in reply, and once he had said, 'That's grand red hair your auntie's got.'

He might let her sit for a while in the warm farm kitchen. Already in imagination she could see his thin form in the horsehair rocking chair; his long, sad face like a horse's face, the small round hat he always wore in the house, and the dark trousers pushed into the tops of his heavy boots. He had a yellow moustache almost like a shelf above his mouth, with two brown, drooping ends.

The snow stung her rosy face, gradually paling it. The fingers that grasped the milk jug were almost without feeling. It seemed a long, long way to the farm.

At last she reached it. The dogs, who knew her, neither barked nor looked out of the doors of their cold kennels. The house was dark and the door fast shut. Through the window she could see the last dying spark of a fire, but there was no sign of a human being.

She felt angry with Mr Jepson for being out. He would have left the milk in a can for her inside the milk house, where the cooler was. It would be so hard to pour the milk from the can to the jug in the dark, and so cold, too; but Mr Jepson did not like her to take the can. The shelf was high, and there were always things in the way, but in spite of her chilled hands she managed to make the transference. Through the darkness, she heard the sound of moving animals. There were all the cows, warm in the byre. And Mr Jepson would have brought the horse Bobbie in from the fields to the stable. It was too cold to leave anything outside this night.

She thought of the cows, of the way they moved their thin hind legs, slip-slopping in and out of the gutter; of the unbearable heat that rose from their bodies and almost pressed you backwards. And as she fastened the stiff door, she felt that it would be very nice indeed to warm her hands on a cow.

The way home seemed endless, and snow began to cake in hard lumps on her boot heels, making her progress still slower. Unheeded, little trickles of milk ran down the jug sides. Was there nothing else in the world but the cold, the snow, the wind and the darkness? She began to make little whimpering noises, yet she plodded on, pressing the milk jug tight between her numbed hands. And the whole of her small spirit resolved itself into the determination to keep on struggling at all costs, and to go forward; as if by so doing she would be rewarded in some way undreamed of up to now.

THUNDER SHOWER

Two girls stood sheltering under the sunblind of a shop where raincoats, bathing suits, and rubber shoes were sold, waiting for the heavy June thunder shower to stop. Sometimes they looked in the windows of the shop at the bright and frail-looking articles, noting the prices from habit, but without any particular interest.

The elder one was tall, thin, and fair. She had a few made-up curls showing under her hat, and she was hoping that the shower would not make the air damp enough to straighten them. At the same time, she was feeling sorry for her friend, who was in very great trouble.

The friend, Olive, was trying to push her desperate thoughts as far into the background as possible. She was short and dark, with light, steely-grey eyes, a fair complexion, and thin lips. She wore clothes that were dark blue in colour, going shabby, but well brushed. Some time ago she had sent her watch to be mended, but did not care to call for it, as she had now no money to spare. Yet she kept looking anxiously at her wrist. Each time she looked, the other girl, whose name was Lilian, said, 'Don't worry, Olive, we can hear the Town Hall chimes.'

The two girls were waiting for a mounted policeman called Austin Fryer, who was the cause of Olive's trouble. He would be out of the stables by five o'clock, and she had written and told him that she must see him, and that she would be waiting in front of the White Café from five o'clock to half-past. The White Café was just across the road. They had waited there for a few minutes, until the heavy shower had driven them to take shelter under the awning of the rubber shop.

'Do you think I ought to go?' Lilian asked nervously. 'He mightn't come if he sees two of us.'

'Don't go,' said her companion, in a hard, level voice.

Secretly, each girl was convinced that the man would not turn up, yet to stand there waiting for him was at least to be doing something. Time was going so quickly. It was over two months since Olive had met him last.

The drenching shower, breaking unexpectedly into the sunny afternoon, had driven most of the pedestrians from the streets. A tram, bus, or motor car would pass along the gleaming road occasionally. The air was fresh. The two girls could not help smiling faintly now and then, as they saw a sight which appeared funny to them – an immaculately dressed man driving an open car, his face dark with anger, rain running off the back of his hat; or a woman in flimsy clothes stepping unwillingly from a tram into the pelting downpour – yet as soon as they smiled and looked at each other, their faces would alter, become strained, and the smile would vanish.

They were the only two sheltering in that particular place. Inside the shop, it seemed to be very quiet, and the smell of rubber oozed out of the open doorway, permeating the air around them.

Sometimes Olive would open her lips to release fragments of sentences. 'If only everything could be all right again. This would be a lesson to me. For ever. I'd never – ' She started as a cold drop fell on her cheek, and stopped talking to watch the figure of a man running along Cheapside. Lilian thought this might be Austin.

Olive half-closed her eyes and laughed shortly. 'He wouldn't run to see me now,' she said. 'If he comes at all, it'll be when the rain has stopped. He wouldn't care if I waited all the time in the rain. I know that man.'

She said it so bitterly that Lilian stared at her. 'Olive,' she began, 'whatever made you – '

'Oh, shut up,' said Olive. 'I did, and he did, and that's all. And now I'm in this mess. If only I could get out of it.' She clenched her fists and ground her teeth with rage.

'Don't talk so loud, they'll hear you in the shop,' whispered Lilian, giving a scared look into the rubber-scented dimness of the doorway.

'Oh, oh,' breathed the other girl in an ecstasy of misery. 'Somebody's going to hear something soon. I can't bear it much longer. I feel like stopping people in the street and making them listen to me while I tell them all about it.'

Even while she said it, she could imagine the answering voices. 'This is what comes of curiosity. You should have been a good girl. You've had your fun, now you must pay for it. You knew what you were doing.' All lies. She had had no fun, neither had she quite known what she was doing. It seemed to her that she was only reaching out towards some satisfaction which she never really got. She thought that she had been cheated.

Lilian turned round uncertainly, and began fingering some coats which were hanging from a hook at the side of the window. Their bright colours were attractive. In August, she would be going to Blackpool for a week. She pictured herself walking down the promenade in one of these coats, looking attractive and carefree. Should she get a blue or a green? They were very cheap, she must try to get one before August.

'Come and look in the window, Olive,' she said animatedly. 'Aren't these coats lovely?'

Olive walked up and stared at the goods displayed, but she did not see them. She had begun to think about Austin Fryer. How pleased she had been the first time he had leaned down from his perfectly groomed horse to talk to her. And the first day he had arranged to meet her, she remembered that, too. She was late. He had stood waiting for her for five minutes, and when she went towards him, he was staring fixedly across the road, a frown marking the space between his eyes. Even when she spoke to him, the frown did not disappear, so that she felt compelled to say, with forced brightness, 'I'm sorry I'm late.' That was a bad beginning.

He was a big, heavy man, with strongly marked features and a humourless expression. He was moody. He had not much to say, and she had not much, either, to say to him. A kind of magnetism chained them when they were together that grew powerless as soon as they parted.

He took her home to see his mother, a little bent old woman with a high, squeaking voice, and eyes heavy with smouldering jealousy.

'This is Olive, mother,' he said. 'We're courting.'

'Are you?' piped the old woman, grinning slyly. 'Well, then, I hope you'll court for ever.' This was her greeting.

Austin was her last remaining son. She adored him, and waited on him like a slave, cleaning all his things, washing his razor after him, even once a week making him sit down on a low chair at her side while she manicured his fingernails.

She took an instant dislike to Olive, and whenever she could, would push the girl into a corner, nudge her with a sharp elbow, and say, 'What do you want with him, eh? He's thirty-five and still single. You won't get him. Others have tried. Ha ha!'

She was always smiling and shaking her head knowingly, as she sat opposite them at the tea table. When she passed Olive a cup of tea, she would say for a joke: 'There's many a slip 'twixt cup and lip,' and she would throw a smile to her son.

Austin would sit heavily in his chair, looking down at his plate, torn between fondness for his mother and desire for this girl. If she said too much, he would sometimes growl, 'Can't you shut that everlasting nitter-natter?' Once he got up so violently that his cup of tea was spilt over the clean cloth, snatched his cap and walked out of the house, shouting, 'Come on,' over his shoulder to Olive.

'That's right,' his mother chirped, folding her hands and watching the tea soak into the cloth. 'Go after him. Hurry up and catch him before he slips through your fingers.' And Olive, hating to be left alone with her, went.

The Town Hall clock chimed the quarter. The girls looked at each other, as if to say, 'He'll never come now' or 'We may as well wait.' Lilian spoke comfortingly: 'He might have been kept at the stables.'

'No,' said Olive. 'He always comes out on the stroke. He might be sheltering, that's all. But I think he'll have gone home.'

They moved restlessly. The shower had lasted already twenty minutes, and showed few signs of stopping. The sky had brightened, yet the drops came down heavily and unendingly. Lilian kept putting a furtive hand up to her curls to see if they were lying lank on her cheek. Each time she felt their dry roundness, a contented look dwelt temporarily in her eyes. She stared across at the White Café, and as she looked, remembered how surprised she had been when Olive had first told her about her trouble.

They had met by appointment one evening, after work, and had gone to have some ice cream together. The café they chose was down in a basement, low-ceiled, red-carpeted, and close-smelling. There were thick pink shades over the few lamps. Four young, fresh-looking men on a raised platform played short, loud tunes, which sounded like jug ajug ajug jug, jug ajug ajug jug, many times repeated. They felt drowsy and relaxed, yet inwardly excited by the loud music.

They had eaten their ices, and were sitting talking to each other, their elbows on the table, when Olive said, smiling stiffly: 'Lil, I have been a fool. I've been such a fool. What shall I do?'

Lilian felt startled and sorry at the same time. In a flash she took in her friend's meaning; it could only be one thing, or she would not have said it in the way she did, as if anxious to rid herself of some horrible dread by exposing it. But it would not do to let Olive think she had jumped to that conclusion. 'There are other ways of being a fool,' she thought; and she gave her friend a questioning look.

Olive broke in before the other girl could say anything. 'Yes.' She nodded. Her voice sank to less than a whisper. 'But, of course, I can't be sure. I'd better wait.'

At the same time, she knew that what she feared was a certainty.

'Have you told *him*?' asked Lilian, after a short silence.

'Well, I did just mention it.' Olive's voice rose a little hopefully. 'But he said that *that* was an absolute impossibility.'

'Yes, they always do,' said Lilian. She did not say this from experience, but as a result of workroom confidences. 'But it keeps on happening all the same.'

For a time they listened to the band, and thought. Lilian moved her toes round and round. She had some new shoes on, and they were tight. She kept looking at her friend's eyes, and admiring them. The irids were so clear as to look transparent.

'Didn't he say anything else?'

Olive gave a short laugh. 'You needn't expect a wedding,' she said. 'The last thing he'll do is ask me to marry him. He says, "Whatever would my mother think if I had to disgrace her?" He says, "Can't you go to one of those women – the town's full of them." As if I should know any of "those women" whoever they are!' At the same time, she looked at Lilian anxiously, as if she might know somebody, or something.

'There is a funny sort of woman lives not far from us,' Lilian said in a troubled voice. 'You might find out –'

In the end, Olive had nerved herself to knock at a door, feeling that a thousand eyes were spying on her from neighbouring windows. An old woman took her hand and half pulled her inside. 'Do ye want your fortune tellin', dearie, or is it somethin' else?' There was something the matter with her throat, and she could only speak in a croaking whisper. The house was low and dark, and smelt of mice and earth.

Full of dread, Olive turned to go, but the woman pushed her into a chair, smiling and saying, 'Now, dearie, tell me all about it. You're not the first, and you'll not be the last, mercy me, no. A bad thing for my trade if you was. Have ye got a few shillin's for an old woman? That's right. I'll 'ave some water boiling in 'alf a tick. No one can say I aren't clean. Take off your coat and let me put it over your head. There's nothing to shiver about, lass. We'll soon 'ave ye smilin' again.'

The old hag had wheedled the last penny from her purse, so that she had to walk home, trembling and sick, convinced that nothing would come of her visit but the loss of her few shillings. In this, she had been right.

At last she heard of a man 'properly qualified, but down on his luck', who could, with certainty, 'make everything all right again'; but he wanted five pounds.

'Where do you think I could get five pounds?' she had asked Lilian. The money seemed as remote to the girls as the moon.

'You ought to write to Austin and tell him you want it,' Lilian had answered.

Olive thought of her lover, and of his behaviour since he had heard her news. Although he said that he did not believe it, he had reluctantly given her ten shillings to go again to the old woman in Primrose Street, and was angry because they had been wasted.

'You were a fool,' he said, 'to give her the money first.'

'Do you suppose she'd have done anything without it?' she had retorted spiritlessly.

But it was true that the old woman had only wanted money, and that she was more amused than anything by the girl's condition. When she found that nothing else was to be had, she had broken into a shout of laughter. 'What's it matter to you?' she croaked. 'You'll 'ave to come down a peg or two, me lady, and ask the chap to wed ye. And in twenty years ye'll be playin' smash because your own lass'll go an' do the same thing. I know!' Suddenly she changed her tone and said in a wheedling voice: 'If you *could* get 'old of a few more shillin's we'll try somethin' else. It'll be 'ard for me to get, an' I'll 'ave to walk me old legs off, but I'd do a lot for you, dearie.'

'I can't get another penny,' Olive said. The old woman had a few fresh flowers in a vase on the table. They looked out of place in the dirty hovel. The girl fixed her eyes on them, and thought, 'I wish it was last year.'

The old woman put her lips close to the girl's ear. 'You want to frighten 'im,' she whispered. 'You 'aven't any sense at all. Stubborn as a mule, you are. Your sort always comes off worst.'

So Olive had written: 'Dear Austin, – Should like to see you tomorrow night. Shall wait outside the White Café until half-past five. – Your friend, Olive. P.S. – It is very important. I hope you can be there.'

The rain had by now lessened. The road was shining; people were leaving shelter, and one by one crossing its clear-cut blackness. With heavy strokes, the bells told the half-hour. The two girls still stood under the awning. As the clock struck, Lilian patted her friend's shoulder.

'We'll just stay a few minutes yet,' she said consolingly; 'but if he isn't here by five and twenty to, I shall have to go.'

Olive kept looking up the street down which the man might come. Her face was growing desperate. She twisted her fingers. 'Oh, Lil,' she whimpered, 'if only I knew where I could get five pounds. Just five pounds.' Her lover and the little he had meant to her faded from her consciousness.

Lilian looked round uneasily. 'I'll really have to go now, Olive,' she said. All this was not her fault. She became a little impatient. Olive ought to have got round Austin, she thought, even threatened to tell his mother. Lilian felt that she would have acted quite, quite differently.

'Cheer up, Olive,' she said with forced brightness. 'I'll be seeing you again soon.'

'All right,' Olive answered quietly.

Lilian left the other girl standing under the awning, her eyes staring at the façade of the White Café, her hands clasped in front of her. The sun had come out again, and was whitening the water in the gutters and the hollows of the road. A horse slipped on the cobbles and was shouted at by the man in the cart behind. Fresh flowers outside a florist's shop filled the clean air with scent.

As she walked along, Lilian felt exhilaration glowing through her whole body. There was so much to look forward to. Saturday had been wasted, but there was all Sunday to follow. Blackpool in seven weeks, the new coat, sunshine. Her lips parted in a smile.

She turned round, shaded her eyes, and looked down the long road towards the shop with the red-striped awning. Nobody stood there now.

PRODIGAL'S HOLIDAY

'Cyril's coming!' the children shouted.

'Sirra's coming!' Even the fat baby of two, who had never seen or heard of Cyril before, ran about shouting it after them.

It was warm and still. The plum tree stood with its narrow leaves half shut, and seemed to press white blossom and black twigs into the very sky itself. You could hardly remember how it had shrunk naked from the wind last autumn, and bent low to the parlour window, as if it were screaming to come in, like one of the children.

The plum tree had always been there. If you had asked one of them, 'Who planted the plum tree?' he would have answered, 'Nobody. It has always been there.' Or another of them might have said 'Gaud,' it not being polite to say 'God' outright. But they would have looked at you a little contemptuously.

One of the boys lay on the lawn with his arms outstretched and his eyes shut, pretending to be crucified. Every minute or two the fat baby Mona climbed unsteadily over his rigid body, echoing breathlessly, 'Sirra's coming.' As soon as anything else took her attention, she would be off. Alec was supposed to be looking after her, but as usual he was relying on mother to knock on the window if anything went wrong. The child might manage to unfasten the gate and get out into the road. It was fortunate that the gate creaked very badly. 'Yaw!' it shrieked if anybody touched it.

The postman had only just gone, but the letter had been opened and read, and the excitement had spread from the far attic to the garden gate. Even father had been visibly pleased. He loved the whole dozen of his children, never demonstratively – they could not remember his having kissed them – but deeply.

Cyril was coming home! Cyril, the first-born, the tiny, skinny scrap who had come into the world weighing just over five pounds. What a difficult baby he had been, rejecting every kind of food offered him by his thin, patient girl-mother. One day he had decided to stop his constant wailing and die. Mother had often told the story. She was nursing Cyril when she heard him give a sudden sharp sigh, and fold his blue eyelids over his bluer eyes. An expression of peace, which had never before been there, came over his small face. Mother's heart beat quickly, though she was not really afraid. She knew he was going to die. All her own brothers and sisters had died young, and she remembered that when they were dead, she used to go and sit on the step in the street and cry, and sometimes a kind neighbour would give her a penny. 'Our new baby's dead,' she would sob, and even strangers would stop and stroke her hair, and give her a penny. She got quite used to it.

Now she sat on the lowest step, a girl of seventeen, a long plait of pure golden hair hanging over each shoulder, holding the puny infant on her knee; waiting with an expression half pride, half sorrow, for father to come home.

As soon as the door opened, she looked up. 'I think the baby's dead,' she said in an awed voice.

Father snatched Cyril out of her arms. He did not even wait to take his hat off. 'Get some brandy,' he cried in a high, hoarse voice; and mother, vaguely frightened, had brought some brandy.

Father had not gone to bed that night. By sheer force of will, it seemed, he had made the child live. And afterwards, he had said to mother sternly, 'In this house, babies don't die.' She had looked at him meekly, and gone on having baby after baby just to please him, and keep him quiet. But sometimes even she got angry, having them for nearly thirty years. A child never got to be three before there was another one.

Cyril had grown up, thin and small always, but not delicate. He had a long back, and fairly short legs; his blue eyes were set in a face red-brown, a little like a Red Indian's.

He had become moody, because a younger brother had sprung up, tall and handsome, with a mop of yellow hair and a sneering lip. Though this boy was some years his junior, he could almost beat Cyril in their frequent fights.

'Stop that noise!' mother would cry, fiercely pressing her youngest to her breast, as if to protect it from the sound of conflict. 'Can't you boys live without quarrelling? It's like being in a dog kennel here!'

She did not quite mean that, but the boys would try not to

look at each other for a few minutes. The instant one looked at the other, the same spark of hatred seemed to set them both alight. Once, after they had been separated, the younger one had shouted derisively, 'It's a damn pity mother ever found that brandy.'

Now that was Cyril's cherished story. He had felt himself important in the world because of it, and always liked to hear mother tell it. He would fix his blue eyes on his mother's hazel ones, sitting in front of her on a hassock, a hand curled round either knee. Now and again he would prompt her: 'And then father said – and then you said – '

Father took the younger brother upstairs and thrashed him.

The thrashing seemed to bring everything to a head. Next morning, both of the boys had run away. How quiet everything was! Mother kept saying, 'They'll come back. I shouldn't worry.' But she did worry all the same.

At the end of the week a dirty letter without a stamp on it came from the younger one. He had only got to Hull, where he had tried to stow away on a Norwegian steamer, and been kicked off, and his courage left him. He wanted father to come and bring him home. When father got him home, he was surprised and pleased to know that Cyril had run away too. 'I wouldn't have left if I'd known he'd go,' he said. 'We shall have a bit of peace in the house now.'

'Oh, you bad boy,' his mother wept, holding a baby in her arms. 'You don't know what you're saying.' For she loved Cyril.

Year after year had gone by, and Cyril had never once come back. They had had letters from him, letters from different parts of the world. Sometimes, in a fit of generosity, he sent money home. 'Get yourself a little present, mother, a silk dress or something.' She thanked him by letter, but she never got a silk dress, as the money always trickled away in small things: new clothes for the babies; wedding feasts for the girls, who insisted on marrying early, for love; little gifts for their babies. But she tried to rescue shillings from the housekeeping money. . . . 'Next year, I'll really get a dress, a black one.' She was growing older; her yellow hair was whitening imperceptibly. And she never bought the dress after all.

Now Cyril was coming, coming this very day. Though it was early, she was already baking pies. She had some American apples on the table, and one very small basin of forced gooseberries. Her face was flushed. The oven was not drawing so well, and she had been pushing pieces of wood beneath it, praying secretly as she pushed each piece, 'Draw, oven. Please do. Cyril's coming.' But instead of flames roaring up the oven flue, faint puffs of smoke rolled languidly into the chimney and vanished. There was no draught at all.

She wore a long white apron, shaped and fastened over her now comfortable hips; a washed-out pink blouse, and a white dust-cap with two wings, a little askew. Sometimes there was a faint crackling sound as she moved the rolling pin backwards and forwards; she had pushed Cyril's letter inside her blouse, like any schoolgirl. She felt like a girl again, her thoughts having gone back to the evening when she had held the sickly child on her knee and waited for her husband to come home.

How quickly life was going, when one thought about it.
Cyril would be over thirty now. She thought of the way he
used to sit in front of her, his eager mouth open, his bright
eyes set a little crookedly in his small face, his hands like paws
spread over his knees. He had looked immature, as if there
had not been enough material to form him. Oh, how could he
have run away from home and stayed away all those years!

She looked out of the window and saw some of the children
in the garden. The youngest had picked up something, and
was looking at it gravely, preparatory to putting it in her
mouth. Alec was still lying crucified, his face contorted with
imaginary pain. She knocked sharply, and called to him to look
after Mona; but it was a long time before he opened his eyes.

'Mo-na,' he called, dragging out the syllables. 'Come to
Alec.'

'No!' she said, stamping with a plump foot on the grassy
path. 'No!' So he had to pull himself up reluctantly and go to
her. As soon as she saw him rise, she ran off shrieking with
laughter to hide behind some holly bushes on the back path,
her eyes tight shut, her hands clenched near her ears. Oh, she
was happy! 'You can't find me, you *can't* find me,' she chanted,
and waited a second or two. Then she threw down the piece
of dirt, and went running after the grey cat from next door.
''moky, 'moky,' she cried, but with slow dignity the cat crept
through a small hole in the hedge.

Then she ran indoors, and tried to pick up a handful of
green gooseberries. Somebody seized her wrist and her booty
dropped to the floor. 'Aoo,' she wailed, watching two of the
tiny berries which took a long time to roll from her curled

hand. And then again she was out on the lawn. climbing over Alec and singing 'Sirra's coming.'

Slowly the morning crept on. Every time you looked out of the door you could see new shoots of pale green coming up somewhere. The sooty-looking black of the trees was almost covered. It was good to see the early plum-blossom, and to think of the time when everything would be clothed heavily in green, and bees would sway upon the lupin stalks. What would be happening then?

Father had gone to meet Cyril. He had been gone a long time; they wondered what could be keeping him. The pies were baked, there was a smell of meat cooking in the oven, and two big black pans stood upon the rib of the fire grate, as well as the two on the gas stove in the scullery.

'Have you lit the parlour fire?' mother asked Dora anxiously; then she added crossly, 'Put that pin down.' Dora was always poking between her teeth with a pin. She had several holes there, but she could not go to the dentist's as there was not enough money available to pay him, and unless mother had all the money ready, she would not embark upon an enterprise. 'You'll have to see the dentist,' she said in a harassed way, and then, happily, she forgot about it.

Dora and Mona tripped and fell on the rug near the large black pans, and somebody screamed. They both cried, and mother ran to scold them, so that when the gate sounded its warning 'Yaw!' nobody heard it but Alec, who ran to the door.

Father was coming up the path, and another man was by his side; a small man with a rather dirty, loose blue raincoat on. Alec looked at a pair of very bright blue eyes.

'Cyril?' he asked in an excited, squeaky voice.

Cyril had all his luggage in a black canvas bag, such as sailors carry. Indeed, he had just come off a tramp steamer, where he had a job as cook. He had a fixed smile on his face, a little too bright to be natural. He had apparently been drinking, and had persuaded father to have a drink or two. How had he managed that?

Alec did not know this, but he felt that there was something strange about Cyril. He did not like it when Cyril stared at him and said, still smiling, 'Er – one of the kids?'

By this time the whole family had come to the door and overflowed on to the path, and Cyril was in mother's arms. As soon as mother smelt the beer on his breath she stiffened, but Cyril had forgotten mother's ways, and that when she was angry she stiffened. He kept on smiling and looking at everybody, and exclaiming.

When they were inside, mother looked at father in a hostile way. The years had changed them, and she was now the dominant partner. She had decided that he was responsible for Cyril's condition, though that was not true. Father tried to stare gravely back at her, but beer did not agree with him, so he began to hiccup. Tears came into her eyes. She fussed around Cyril, calling him 'lovey' and pulling at his greasy raincoat with her delicate fingers.

She saw the dark hair again, growing low in his neck as it had always done. Some of his teeth were discoloured, and his hands were stained deep brown, their nails cracked and blackened. A lump came into mother's throat as she saw these things. In Cyril's cheek something beat quickly;

his smiling lips trembled, then fixed themselves into a grimace.

'Have I got a room?' he asked, as if he were seeking to escape. Mother took him upstairs, and shut the bedroom door behind them.

When she had gone downstairs again, Cyril stood near the window. He looked as if he were still smiling, but tears were following one another down his hardened cheeks. 'Well, it's home,' he was thinking. And in one way, it appeared to him to be in no way different from anywhere else. There was the plum tree on his left. He did not notice that it had grown at all, indeed, it seemed rather less to him, because he had thought it was a very giant of a plum tree, years ago.

At dinner time, Cyril surprised the family by eating hardly anything; and it was all good, so good that Alec had what he called 'three servings of the first.' The dinner was served straight from the pans on to the plates. If you wanted any more, you just got up from the table, and went from pan to pan with your plate. Thus everything was always hot, but the things were much harder to wash up afterwards, because the vegetables dried on the pan sides.

After dinner, Cyril decided to go back to town with father. 'Well, of course' – mother forgave him – 'of course he'll want to go with father.' All the same, she was not satisfied in her own mind. The small thought persisted, 'He might have stayed with me for the first few hours.' He smelt strange to her, but at times looked the same as he had done years ago.

Just before he went out, he said to one of the girls: 'By the way, I have a bunch of dirty clothes, do you think you could

81

wash them for me?' It was Dora he spoke to. 'Oh, yes!' she cried enthusiastically, as though she loved washing clothes, 'I'll look after them!'

'That's a regular girl,' he said, giving her an awkward kiss. She blushed as though a stranger and not a brother had kissed her.

What a lot of clothes he had, and how dirty they were, she thought. They had all sorts of names and initials on, not his own. Everybody wondered how he had come across them. It was hard work getting them clean, but they did it, talking about him all the time. The girls were wondering if he would take them to the theatre, and buy them some chocolates. They had already decided what to wear.

Mother smacked Alec's face for grinning and saying suddenly, 'He-he, isn't he funny?' After she had clouted him, she said grimly, 'Not half as funny as you are. Your ears are *black*, go wash them.' As he scraped his ears until they were scarlet, Alec muttered to himself, 'But he *is* funny. He looks like a little Tich.' He had seen a picture in an old magazine on which was printed 'Little Tich.'

Cyril came home in the middle of the afternoon with a large fish under his arm. It was a sort of present, but this was quite the wrong sort of present. Mother had been hoping that he would give her a little money; not as much even as this great fish had cost, but just enough to enable her to buy the extra food. She was grieved when she saw the fish. They seemed to be eating fish for days afterwards, and Cyril did not help them at all. After one little piece, he did not take any more. It was just the same as at the first meal, he ate next to nothing.

He asked about the brother for whose sake he had left home, and who was now married, but would not bother to go to see him. He spent most of his time out, away from the house, and many times came home late. He wore his perpetual glassy smile, and if mother waited up for him, he seemed not to understand her look of dumb love. He would merely say, 'I don' wan' anything eat thang you,' and go upstairs to bed. He would never talk of his life, or of the places he had seen. Sometimes he would say to Alec, 'I would tell you a lot, like a book, see? But it's all the same, anywhere. Beer and gals and grub. And work between times. See?'

A neighbour saw him in town once, swaying along, his arms around the waists of two women. They were taller than he was, but he strutted along, talking away to them, boasting, swaggering. They did not seem to mind being with him, or think he was funny. They knew he had some money in his pocket.

The one who had seen him told mother. She smiled gently, and pretended that it was a very good joke indeed; but it hurt her. The sisters heard too and they were angry, and looked at Cyril without smiling each time they saw him. They were beginning to think the house would be better without him. Their visit to the theatre had not taken place, he had bought nothing for them; they behaved coolly towards him.

But at last, Alec liked him. Sometimes Cyril let him sit on the bed while he got ready. He liked to watch this strange brother wash his feet in cold water, and cut his horny toenails with a sharp knife. He liked to twirl the string of the black canvas bag which hung from the catch on the wardrobe door, and to hear Cyril croak 'Hop along now,' when he was going to turn the light out. It made everything seem different at home, as if there were two worlds in the house. He could be in one or the other by merely opening a door.

Instead of asking her son for money, mother put less and less food on the table, yet she always asked anxiously, 'Would you like an egg? Can the children get you anything from the shop?'

Cyril would say, 'I guess this'll suit me,' and he would eat a little bread and butter, and go out.

One morning as he sat in bed drinking the cup of tea that mother always took up for him, he said, looking at the wall opposite the bed-foot, 'I'm going back today.'

Mother put a quick hand to her mouth, but before she could say anything, Cyril thrust the empty cup towards her. She went slowly downstairs and told everybody. The others felt as if they had been hanging by the hair for a long time, and that somebody had just come and cut them quietly down. They began to talk loudly and unnaturally. 'Had we better say goodbye, or will he be here when we get back tonight?'

In a few minutes Cyril came downstairs, ready, and with all his clothes packed. He was going to town with father; father would see him off, he said.

'But where are you going?' asked mother anxiously, wringing her hands.

'I'm not a kid, mother,' he answered softly.

Alec thought that he looked like a mouse trying to find a hole in the trap, and burned to aid him. Cyril did not need his help. 'Well, so long,' he said, giving mother a hasty kiss. 'I'll be slipping in some other time, see?' His bright glance roved round the kitchen, noticing the cups with the raised blue forget-me-nots on them, the big brown teapot, the high dresser with the glass knob on its low cupboard, the etching of the highwayman in a dark corner, the hair springing from the girls' heads, the parted lips and white teeth of his baby sister.

And he was gone before mother could get out the words, 'What about your breakfast, what about your breakfast?' Mother's face was filled with horror and remorse as she thought of all the food she had not given him, all the things she had not done for him.

A few minutes afterwards, Mona lowered herself carefully down the steps, holding a jammed crust in her hand. She wanted to play with Alec before he went to school. All the others were busy talking, father had gone, and mother was up in her bedroom. Alec was lying face downwards on the lawn, wishing that he had shouted 'Write to *me*!' after his brother. Life seemed to be growing stale. It was the same sort of day as that on which Cyril had come, but the plum blossom had withered and fallen; and now the apple trees were covered with pink.

When the little girl saw her brother lying there, she began to laugh, and ran towards him waving her bread, and shouting cheerfully, as if she had remembered something. 'Sirra's coming, Sirra's coming!' He kept quite still, not noticing her, so she went and stood under an apple tree, and waited impatiently for the petals to fall on her up-turned face.

SOMETHING FOR TOMORROW

Joseph Elstreet, a small, spare, hard-working man, died at the age of fifty-eight and left a widow of thirty-seven, a daughter of eighteen, and two hundred pounds in the bank. There was also a house, the mortgage on which was nearly paid, but as it was in the widow's name, she reckoned that as hers already. He had died suddenly, on his way to work one morning. His wife and daughter were naturally upset, cried a good deal, and wore the deepest black clothes; but like a couple of daisies that had been trodden on by an unkind foot, soon regained their bloom and appeared, if anything, to have gained by the experience.

Mrs Elstreet was short, plump, dark-haired, and had a fresh pink and white complexion. She wore a fringe, and took great care of her fingernails, because twenty years ago a young man had told her that they were quite pretty. Her eyes were a beautiful mixture of hazel and violet, not dimmed in any way by her years. She was easygoing, inclined to untidiness, and liked to wear very slack-fitting shoes in the house. Sometimes the shoes had five or six holes in them, on the top and underneath, but she went on wearing them for comfort, until some stranger's scrutiny shamed her into getting another pair.

Her daughter Amy was small, fair, rather colourless and quiet, resembling her father in looks. She had prim little lips and greenish eyes, and liked to dress in dark blue frocks with a white collar and cuffs. She was always washing these in the bathroom, starching them and taking them into the kitchen to iron. Her mother laughed about this, but was secretly elated by her daughter's pride in her personal appearance. The two of them got on very well together without being demonstrative.

They had a lodger in the house, called Miss Costello. She had been with them for some years. She was tall, with ginger-coloured hair, a pale, thin face, and very bony hands. She wore gold-rimmed eyeglasses and talked down her nose. She had her own room, and cooked her meals in that room. Most of the day she was out, as she had a job in town; in the evenings she often sat with the family. She liked Mrs Elstreet, but between her and Amy there was a kind of secret feud. They did not care to look at each other, and rarely let their glances meet, except in annoyance or contempt.

After her husband's death, Mrs Elstreet went to sleep in her daughter's room, so that there was now a spare bedroom. She had decided to take another lodger, a man this time, because a man would be able to pay more. She did not want to touch the two hundred pounds that had been left to her, possibly it might be needed on a more serious occasion. There was Miss Costello's money, not much, it was true, but paid weekly; and Amy's small wages – she was a junior clerk –

and Mrs Elstreet told herself that it was a case of another lodger or she herself would have to go out to work.

She did not want to do this, as there was not much at which she was particularly apt except cooking. There was nothing she could not cook, once she had made up her mind to do it. Every fourth Sunday she would ask Miss Costello most ceremoniously to dinner, as if to tempt her away from her own frugal existence, her 'treats' of fourpenny tins of spaghetti or sardines. Much as she liked it, Miss Costello would not be wiled into becoming a boarder. As it was, she saved a few shillings a week and got one free dinner a month. She had never been ill and did not see any reason for changing.

About a month after her husband's death, Mrs Elstreet was told of a young man who was looking for rooms. He wanted a bedroom and a sitting room, most meals and attendance, and was willing to pay well for them. He was travelling for some large London firm or other in the north, and had a small car. He would be glad if there was a garage to the house, but that, of course, was not absolutely necessary if he could find one quite near.

Mrs Elstreet rushed home full of hope to tell Amy and Miss Costello. Feverishly they turned out the front room, pushing the writing desk into the recess near the fireplace and moving the carpet round, worn side to the window. Even Miss Costello helped, rolling her black sleeves above her bony elbows, doing everything that needed to be done with a wash-leather and a bowl of aired water.

'Of course, we mightn't *get* him,' Mrs Elstreet said, standing on the stepladder to dust the picture rail, which was high. 'But it's always as well to be prepared. Mr Jarratt told him about the rooms and he said he might call any time.' She knelt on the top step, clutching her duster firmly and throwing agitated glances around the room. 'I think I'll take poor Joe's photograph out,' she went on. 'Perhaps it'll depress him.'

The photograph of Joseph was an old one, taken many years ago, and now faded. She unhooked it. 'Bring the picture we got with the coupons out of the kitchen, Amy, the little one,' she called over her shoulder. 'I'll put this upstairs in our room. We'll always want daddy.' She sniffed as she climbed down the ladder, tenderly holding the photograph.

'Don't be long,' called out Miss Costello anxiously. She was terribly afraid that she was doing most of the work that was being done. She glanced with some venom at Amy who had hung the picture and was now languidly cleaning the already bright fire-irons in comfort near the fire. 'You could get a cloth and polish these after me,' she suggested, tightening her lips.

'Sorry, my hands are all sticky,' Amy replied, turning her head away daintily.

'You could wash them.'

Amy hummed a tune, and slowly pushed a piece of flannel through a hole in the top of the tongs.

Just as they had finished the room, a loud knock came at the front door.

'Who can be here at this time of night?' asked Miss Costello. They were drinking cocoa and eating some home-made biscuits. The clock struck half-past ten. They were all tired and dishevelled, even Amy did not look so spruce as usual.

'You go, Amy,' said Mrs Elstreet, wiping a ring of cocoa from around her mouth with a handkerchief. 'Keep the door on the chain at first.'

Amy went up the passage and opened the front door wide. Her mother and Miss Costello could not look out of the kitchen, as they would have been seen immediately by the visitor, but they sat in their chairs, tense and listening.

They heard a man's voice; then Amy said, 'Just a minute.' She ran down the passage, put her head round the door, and said, 'It's that man about the rooms. Shall I let him in?' Her face was flushed, and her eyes glowed. 'He is nice!'

Her mother's mouth and eyes opened wide in surprise.

'What a time to call,' said Miss Costello in a chill, disapproving voice.

Mrs Elstreet jumped up briskly. 'Wait here, Amy, I'll let him in,' she said. Nobody was going to tell her what to do in her own house. She closed the kitchen door behind her. The two who were left sat there, not looking at each other, Amy petulant and Miss Costello grim, listening to the pleasant murmur of voices in the next room. Footsteps went up the stairs, lingered in the back bedroom, came down again, went into the front, ended in the passage; and the door was softly closed.

Her face pink and brimming over with happiness, Mrs Elstreet dramatically flung open the kitchen door. 'He's fetching his things and coming over tonight,' she announced breathlessly.

'What a strange time to come,' said Miss Costello, slowly drinking dregs of cold cocoa. She sat there thinking wearisome thoughts about teeth and dressing gowns while the other two rummaged for sheets and pillowslips and ran to make up a bed. Amy was as animated as if it had been eleven o'clock in the morning. 'Do you think he'll be warm enough, or had we better leave another blanket folded at the bottom of the bed? Have we enough bacon? What about butter, mother? If there isn't enough, I'll get up early and slip out before breakfast. What kind of a car has he got, I wonder? D'you think he'll ever take us out in it?'

'I do hope everything will be all right. It'll be nice to have a man in the house again. We can let him use your father's shaving mug if he hasn't one of his own. Perhaps he'll want something to eat before he goes to bed. I'd better ask him.'

The unaccustomed sound of a car stopping at their door sent them both running downstairs. Halfway down, Amy stopped and said with comic dismay, 'Oh, mummy, look at your shoes!' The stockings were sprouting through in places.

'Never mind my shoes,' said her mother, laughing. She turned round to whisper, 'He's going to pay well. No going out to work for your mother now!'

The front door bell rang.

The new lodger, whose name was Max Brazell, quickly made himself at home in the house. He was tallish but thin, inclined to fairness; his hair was brushed straight back from his forehead, and he had grey eyes, a little thick in the lids. He had a habit of half-closing his eyes to smile, and this gave his glance a sort of hidden intimacy. Even Miss Costello was forced to admit that he had great charm. She would watch his lips widen to a lazy smile, looking at him with great pleasure and appreciation, as though he were some actor.

At first, the three women were continually talking about him. It was Mr Brazell this, and Mr Brazell that, but very soon they shortened his name among themselves to Max, and in the end, it was Max that they all called him to his face. He was wonderfully polite to them, but it was always Mrs Elstreet who was loudest in her praise of him. She could not control her tongue very well. When the morning was fine and she was out shopping, she would stop all the friends she met and tell them about Max.

'Oh, yes,' she would say in reply to some question, 'we've got such a nice young man at the house. More like a son' – here a frown would appear on her forehead, as she did not really think that the twelve years' difference in their ages made Max altogether a child – 'than a – than anything else.' She would talk about the things he did; how he had taken her and Amy to Gordale Scar the other Sunday, what a careful driver he was, anything so that she could just stand there talking about him.

Amy was taking evening classes, in leatherwork, it was, and she made some beautiful things. Look, this bag was one. And Max was so kind. He insisted on meeting Amy, and bringing her home in his car. Everything was just lovely. A sparkle would come into the eyes of Mrs Elstreet, and a sort of quivering sigh shake through her.

'Be careful he doesn't turn into a son-in-law,' a friend warned her.

Some of the brightness died out of the little woman's face, then came back again. 'Oh, nonsense,' she said, 'Amy's only a child, and Max doesn't think of her as anything else.' She felt as if she were longing to say, 'Max thinks the most of me!' but she wasn't at all sure. He was so appreciative of her cooking, he noticed if she put on anything new, and complimented her on it; yet he was what she called 'exceedingly proper' in his behaviour.

Many a time she felt that she would love to kiss him on the cheek – just a motherly kiss, she assured herself. But however near she got to him, something always stopped her in time. Once the ice was broken, she felt sure that he would be most affectionate. She needed affection. Poor Joseph had meant very little to her, yet she had always made the most of him. She used to say, 'I don't know whatever you'd do without me, Joe,' because she was longing so much for him to tell her that. But he never did.

She used all her waking moments to devise fresh schemes for the comfort of Max. She would cheerfully make dishes which took hours to prepare, and walk miles to get things from the shops he liked. And when she climbed into bed beside Amy, it was to fall into some dream about him.

Now and then she would pull herself up, and ask herself uneasily how it was going to end. She looked in the glass at her round, fresh face, still without trace of coming wrinkles upon it. There were only one or two grey hairs in her head. Of course, he would never marry her. That was not to be thought of. She would not let him even if he wanted to – or so she assured herself. But – if he could just care for her a little, in more than a friendly way. She was finding it hard to keep under control the overwhelming love which she now felt for him.

Always she had cared for people, and people had not cared for her in the same way. When she used to ruffle Joe's remaining hairs tenderly, he would turn round and say with irritation, 'Aw, let me alone, Minnie.' And Amy had been so self-reliant, even as a baby she had turned away from her mother's constant petting. When Miss Costello had first arrived, she had longed for her to be ill, so that she could nurse and coddle her and earn her gratitude. But Miss Costello was blessed with health.

And now Max had come. Each morning she would call him at a quarter to eight. He liked to have plenty of time to get up. At first he took his breakfast alone, but after a while he had it in the kitchen, with Mrs Elstreet and Amy, and seemed to prefer it that way. If he were going early, he would take Amy down town in his car, but some mornings he sat in the other room and wrote business letters. Miss Costello said that she liked to walk. Her enthusiasm for the young man had died away entirely, and now she looked upon him with covert suspicion.

Mrs Elstreet always liked the mornings best on which he stayed behind. She would clear away the table, singing softly; happy because Max was in call. She never disturbed him, never went near his room, much as she wanted to do so. She had found it better to get up very early indeed, and have the room comfortable for him.

She had discarded all of her easy-fitting shoes, and now went tiptoeing about the house in a pair of court slippers, which had their price, 4s. 10½d, printed deeply upon the soles. These shoes caused her some discomfort, as they were too tight; and she did not like to put her feet high on a hassock because she was always conscious of the pricemark. The point of her big toe wore through the cotton upper before the figures underneath the sole wore off.

She took the smallest rebuff from Max very much to heart. The shadow of a frown on his forehead, a meal not enjoyed, a request unaccompanied by a smile; these things she brooded over all day. Then she would think of something she would be able to do for him tomorrow. She would excel herself, see if she didn't! Tomorrow, all would be different! And she would brighten up and go briskly about the house again, planning wonderful things.

There was a morning when a letter came for Max which troubled him a great deal. He did not say anything for some days, then he told Mrs Elstreet that he would have to leave her shortly, as he had been dismissed by his firm.

This was serious. She was all concern for him. 'You mustn't go, Max,' she told him. 'You will soon get something else.'

'I'll have to go,' he said, giving her a mock-hopeless glance. 'For I haven't a cent in the world. I've never been able to save money, you know.'

He sat at the table, his forehead in his hand, biting at his lower lip. This was Mrs Elstreet's chance. She put her warm hand on his hair. 'You shall not leave this house, Max,' she said tenderly, 'while there is anything in it.' She was exalted by the very touch of his smoothly oiled hair, and could hardly bear to take her hand away. Max did not seem to notice it.

'You really mean that?' he asked. 'Of course,' he went on, his spirits rising, 'I suppose I shall get something else before long, and then I can pay you back. But it's nice to know that you want me, that you won't turn me out.'

He looked at her suddenly, and smiled his most charming smile, prolonging it until time itself seemed to stand still for her.

'I'd do anything in the world for you, Max,' she said in a low, emotional voice.

After she had left him the young man yawned several times, looked about the room with proprietary eyes, lit a cigarette, and then settled down to some thought which made him smile. When the cigarette was smoked, he flicked it into the fire, put a soft cushion behind his head, crossed his legs and fell into a doze.

Day after day, week after week went by, but Max was not able to find anything to do. His car was taken away, so that now he always walked down to meet Amy as she came from her class. And he would try helplessly to do odd jobs about the house.

'Run away, my dear, dear boy,' Mrs Elstreet would say, pushing him gently out by the shoulders. 'You're simply no good in the house.' The feel of his coat beneath her hands would sustain her for hours.

She was finding it hard to live without breaking into her capital. She went out surreptitiously in the dawn to clean offices, and got back home in time to prepare breakfast. She was able to sell some of Amy's beautiful work, but not much, so as soon as she could, she found a job for herself, cooking in a factory canteen. The work was hard and rough, but she met it cheerfully, obsessed all the time by thoughts of Max, feeling that at last she was really doing something to help him.

'The poor boy mustn't get depressed,' she said to herself. She was worried by the fact that he had to get a midday meal for himself until Amy offered to come home two or three days a week and share hers with Max.

'That's a good girl,' her mother said happily. Miss Costello sniffed and said she hoped she would find as much kindness when she needed it. By now she disliked Max so much that she could hardly bear to look at him. She told everybody but Mrs Elstreet and Amy that she was feeling 'rather unsettled at the moment.' The old days of cocoa and biscuits and long, comfortable chats had vanished.

One Sunday, Mrs Elstreet found herself alone in the house with the young man. Amy and Miss Costello had both gone out. Max was sitting in front of the kitchen fire, looking harassed and gloomy, when she came downstairs in her one pretty frock of flowered silk. She had grown a little thinner, and her eyes looked large and sad. The light was poor, and something in the firelight made her appear young – even childish.

'You've done so much for me,' he said to her, looking into the heart of the fire, 'but I want you to do even more. Will you?'

Do a favour for him? Of course she would, any favour. His eyes, a little heavy, were staring at the flickering coals, and comets of light chased each other across their greyness. A few wisps of hair, hardly distinguishable except to her loving eyes, had sprung forward from the fair brushed mass and were moving gently down towards his forehead. There was something of complete dejection in his pose.

He looked up at her, in a pleading way, as she leaned against the kitchen table. 'Whatever you ask, Max,' she said, her heart beating a little unevenly.

'I want you to lend me your money.'

'All of it?' she asked, moving one foot idly.

He nodded his head.

'I knew you'd want it,' she said, with a thin note of pleasure in her voice. 'I've known for days. I drew it all out last Wednesday. Wait, I'll get it for you.'

Like a flash, she was out of the door and running upstairs. In less than a minute she was back again, with a thick brown envelope in her hand. She flung herself down beside his chair and gave him the packet, then she said suddenly, in a trembling voice, 'Kiss me just once, Max.'

Putting her hand behind his neck, she slowly drew down his head, closed her eyes, and pressed her lips against his. Mercifully, she did not see his expression. The kiss passed her like a breath of air. She could not remember it; there was nothing in it of all the things she had meant to convey.

Late that evening the three women, Mrs Elstreet, Amy, and Miss Costello, were sitting having supper together for the first time for some weeks when a slight quarrel occurred. It was over something so small that the cause of it was forgotten, but Amy and Miss Costello stood up from the table, confronting each other, pale, breathing quickly. The girl's face expressed for once all of the contempt which she felt for this elderly, disagreeable woman who had never liked her.

'What I mean by respectable's respectable,' said Miss Costello in her nasal voice, swallowing quickly once or twice. 'You might think I've sat in my room and seen nothing, but I have. First one, and then the other of you.' Various patches of bright red appeared on her face, on her forehead, on her chin, and lastly on her pale cheeks. 'Don't think I'm blind, I'm far from it.' She turned to Mrs Elstreet, her voice full of bitter hatred, and pointed with one bony finger. 'I saw you kissing him today, when you thought everybody was out' – here she turned the accusing finger to Amy who still stood with one hand clutching her chair back – 'but I've seen this sly young thing doing more than that. Oh, I'm staying here no longer. I ought to have gone months ago! Such carryings on, and him a married man!'

She went out of the room, trying to push her gold-rimmed glasses, which were awry, back to the middle of her nose. She kept repeating that she was going in the morning. Before she got to the bottom of the stairs, Amy was after her with the swiftness of an animal. She caught hold of Miss Costello's thick skirt.

'Who says he's married?' she said in a suppressed, nervous voice.

Miss Costello pulled at her skirt. 'Don't touch me,' she cried, setting her face into an expression of rage. 'He is, that's all. I found out long ago. Go ask at his firm, if you need to know.' She looked at Amy piercingly. 'And you do! I can see you do!' she finished, her voice a blend of horror and triumph. She ran heavily upstairs.

Amy went back into the kitchen. Her mother was sitting on

the rug, the flowered dress crumpled around her; one elbow was resting on a wooden chair seat, and her hand was holding her head. Her face was expressionless.

The girl jerked her head. 'She says he's married.'

'She says he's married,' repeated her mother stupidly. They looked at each other in silence for some time, then the older woman said again, 'He's married, Amy. That's bad.'

'He ought to have told us,' said the young girl. All the same, she did not believe it. 'Mother,' she continued gently, kneeling down on the rug, 'don't worry yourself. Come along to bed, I'll see to everything. Come on, mother.'

'I gave him all our money,' Mrs Elstreet said in a low voice, 'but that woman's a liar. He never kissed me.' A look of desolation came into her eyes as she turned towards Amy. The dormant love for her daughter stirred. 'He never kissed me,' she said more firmly, standing up and putting one arm around the girl's shoulder.

They could hear Miss Costello moving about in an agitated manner upstairs. The whole place appeared to them suddenly as unbearable, the wallpaper, the curtains, the staring light, the close quietness of the room.

'Never mind about the money. Never mind about anything,' Amy said. 'Let's go to bed. It's late. Max can let himself in with his key, he'll manage for once. There'll be lots to think about tomorrow.'

But they could not sleep. After a long time Amy touched the older woman's hand gently and said, 'Mother, are you awake? Do you know he hasn't come in yet?' It was three o'clock.

Slowly the two rose, and went to his room, their bare feet pattering side by side over the cold linoleum. The room faced them, chill and empty. A night wind blew the curtain towards them, and that was all.

SPRING DAY AT SLATER'S END

People still take their Sunday walk up the hill to Slater's End, though much of the view is now obscured by the bright new houses which will in their turn grow mellow, crumble, and help to form fresh dust for the quiet green grass to cover. But you can walk higher than any houses have yet gone, climb over a lumpy stone wall, and find yourself on a wild moor, where the sheep shun you and curlews cry; and if you are strong-willed and ready to walk in steep places, you will come quickly to the Nab; and over the Nab – on the wild side, not the sheltered one – is the small, walled cemetery known as Slater's End.

Only the very oldest folk are buried there now. For the road is bad, and they have to be 'walked'; but if they say 'Slater's End', it has to be Slater's End, these old women who still wear their bonnets to chapel, and these old men who are sure of eternal salvation for themselves and eternal damnation for most other people. If they have been harsh to their children and driven them away; if they have oftenest got 'rayther the better side of a bargain'; if they have pinched and saved, and denied themselves and theirs pleasure, Heaven is open to them. They have, at any rate, kept away from the sins of the flesh. Yet long ago, the young were carried here too.

One spring morning – not a Sunday, so they were alone on the road – an old, old man and his granddaughter were walking up the hill. They peered with interest into the gardens of the new bungalows, admiring the neat rows of daffodils, always late in this cold part of the country, which lined the straight, cemented paths.

The little girl had a round, rosy face, direct, wondering brown eyes, and comical little tufts and tails of brown hair which straggled over her cheek. Each time they got in front of her eyes she would say, 'Oh, dear!' and push them back under her hat. But the puffs of wind, which came apparently from nowhere, always dislodged them again. And at length she would cry out, in imitation of some admired elder, 'Grandpa, just look at my ridiculous hair!'

The old man walked at an even pace, tapping the ground every now and then with his stout cherrywood stick. He was glad of the pale, warm sunlight, and of the song of half a dozen larks which grew now louder, now fainter. His eyes and ears and legs were good yet, he thought thankfully. The hair was off the middle of his head; he had a tonsure, surely the most becoming way for a man to lose his hair. If there was some at the front, where you could see it yourself, and some at the back, where other folk could see it, what more could you want?

He had the long face, with its long upper lip, and the tight, grim mouth of the moorland folk. The colour of his eyes was almost washed away, but it had been palest blue, even in his youth. He was dressed in the black suit which he had had for over thirty years, and for overcoat wore a sort of black frock-coat, with two buttons at the back. In the flap of this he carried a spotted red and yellow handkerchief, on which he liked to blow his nose with a loud, challenging sound.

He was of the old breed, yet time had subtly softened him. There was the Post Office, where he drew not only his old-age pension, but also a pension due to the death of an unmarried son in the Army. There were the 'pictures', to which everybody, including his independent daughter, Marion Alice, went. These he resisted with a cunning 'Nay'. And there was the wireless, which even his authority could not keep out of the house. For this he had a secret fondness, but would pretend that he did not care for it when other people were in.

Up the road went the two. Sometimes the little girl took hold of her grandfather's hand, sometimes she ran from his side to pick a flower or a piece of grass; and sometimes they rested for a while, leaning against a wall, both staring dreamily at the opposite hill, which seemed to be lying with its head at rest against the bosom of the cloudless sky. Then off they would go again.

In one garden there was a row of washing hanging on a line, swaying gently. A woman in a white apron and a blue mob-cap came out of a door carrying a creaking basket filled with wet, folded white sheets and towels. She smiled and called out, 'A lovely morning, isn't it?' The child stared back at her, unsmiling, while her grandfather answered solemnly, 'It is, indeed,' and went tapping his way upwards.

When they came to the wall, he climbed over it with stiff legs, and the child threw her roundedness forward and scrambled over. 'Are we going right to the top?' she asked, and went running forward without waiting for an answer. She had seen a lamb, separated from its mother. It was afraid of her, and did not know which way to turn, so it opened its mouth wide and bleated. Silently, with bobbing motion, the old sheep approached, looking at the child with a mixture of menace and fear. She stopped, gazed at the sheep with wide eyes, and ran back to the old man, shouting, 'Grandpa, hide me, hide me quick!' When she looked out from the flap of his coat there was nothing to be seen; the sheep and the lamb were hidden behind a rock. And for a long time she walked quietly.

'Where are we going?' she kept asking. Or, 'Grandfather, what's that?' as they saw a hare, quite near. The old man was absorbed in his thoughts, and did not answer. 'I know. I know; it's a rabbit,' she answered herself. 'A rabbit, a rabbit, hurray, a rabbit!' She jumped over the tufts of hard, rough grass on to the bright green pieces which had been nibbled close, finding a hundred things of interest. She picked up a broken bottle, and for a long time carried a piece of the bluish glass carefully before she tired of it and threw it away.

She ran up to the old man, patting his leg above the knee with her chubby hands. 'Is it far, Grandpa? Is it far to the top?'

'Not so far, now,' he said, 'and then we'll have a rest.' He felt in his pocket, slowly. There was the sound of the crackling of a paper bag, and with difficulty he brought out of it a piece of toffee, which he gave to his little granddaughter, who stood near him with sparkling, expectant eyes, and eager mouth half open. She pushed the toffee into the side of her mouth, and sucked noisily and contentedly.

The way grew steeper, and their walk slower. The morning was perfect. Far below, the busy towns, linked together by twisting white roads, shimmered in the mist of their own smoke, and gave out a faint, faint hum, punctuated by occasional louder noises, such as a hammering clatter in the railway yards, or the sound of a bell chiming the quarter-hour.

They came very suddenly on the top of the hill. There was a triangular platform, sheltered by a large rock twice the height of a man and three times the length of one. It was grassy, but cropped almost to the dust by the sheep. The little girl flung herself down and rolled about like a puppy, and the old man sat on a knoll, resting his chin on cupped hands, his elbows on his knees, his cherrywood stick beside him on the ground.

When the child tired of rolling about, she crept close to her grandfather, picked up the walking-stick, and after having smelt its sweetness until she could sniff no longer, walked about in imitation of the old man, pulling down her mouth severely, tapping often with the stick, and all the time darting bright glances at him from the corners of her eyes.

Although his eyes followed her for a while, his thoughts were in the past. Sixty years it was, or more, since Lily had died. And here he was, up at Slater's End, not many yards from where her bones were lying, remembering not the life which had come between, but that short year when he had known Lily.

He could see her face now as he saw it then. Pale, with just a little colour in her cheeks when the wind put it there. Her hair had been flaxen when she was a baby, she had told him, but it had grown a deep golden brown with the years. She had grey-green eyes with tiny pupils, a large nose, and a pretty, crooked mouth. She had small ears, pressed close to her head, and dressed her hair to show them. She was very thin, so thin that when he thought about her slightness his heart contracted with pain.

She was seventeen when he first saw her. She had known trouble and responsibility already, and these had drawn grave shadows across her face; but as she met him, a beautiful smile had come over her like sunshine, and driven those shadows away.

They had not a great deal to say to each other when first they met, boy and girl in the spinning-mill; and they had plenty of work to do. Yet on every pretext, the boy was down at her end of the room, just to see that she was still all right.

It was a long time, almost six months, before he dare ask her if she would go with him for a walk. 'I don't know,' she had said, in her shy way, 'I'll see.' And he waited for a long time one day, until at last she came.

'I thought you'd have gone,' she told him, breathlessly, when she saw him standing in the shadow of a high wall at the bottom of the mill-master's garden. 'I'd have come before, but I couldn't get out.'

'That's all right,' he said, gruffly. And his heart was crying, 'I'd have waited for you for ever, you beautiful little dove.'

'How d'you like it at the mill, then?'

They strolled along, that first time, talking mainly about their work, and about a little man at the mill called Edgar, who was henpecked, and always getting into trouble. She grew animated, and laughed at her companion's jokes.

'I didn't know you could be funny as well as kind,' she said. And they wondered what the stars really were, and why the moon looked just like it did. And they were silent for a long time, thinking vague thoughts; walking a little apart, happy to be with each other.

They met again and again, but she could not walk so far as on the first night. 'I don't know how it is,' she said. 'I've never felt like this before. I used to be as strong as strong when I was a little 'un.'

One Sunday they arranged to get up early and walk to Slater's End. 'It's grand up there,' he told her, 'with the larks and all. You can see for miles around. Let's hope it won't rain!'

The morning had been perfect, just as this one was. 'We've got to get down in time for me to cook dinner,' she said. That was why they had gone so early. And there were no buses then to carry them halfway up the hill. She had on her best frock of dark green, with a white frill at the neck and wrists. And she had on a little green velvet bonnet. He could see the knot of hair in her neck just as plainly now as he did that day.

She let him take her hand to help her up. Her eyelids were strangely heavy, and not even the touch of the wind put colour in her cheeks. 'I don't know why I'm so tired,' she kept saying. But it did not occur to either of them to forgo the excursion. It had been planned, so it must be carried out.

Up the road they walked. There were no houses there yet, only fields reclaimed from the moorland. The lane became a path, which dwindled away to the merest track. 'I will get to the top,' Lily said, gritting her teeth in determination. When they came to the wall she sat down. 'Let's wait a bit,' she said. 'We've time yet.'

Just such another blue sky, he remembered, with the opposite hill resting its smooth cheek against the sky as it was today. He had put his arm about her shoulders. 'Lily,' he had said, looking down at her, 'Lily.' And then he kissed her.

They had almost raced up to the top of the hill. They laughed and teased one another, and rested breathless on the ridge at the top of the hill. 'Isn't it –? Isn't it –?' They couldn't find a word to say of what they thought about it all. He could hardly look at the distant view, when here was Lily, near him. He wanted to kiss her again. Clumsily he pressed towards her. 'Lily, lass?' he questioned.

But as the boy looked towards her, terror came over him. She had leaned forward, her eyes were closed, and bright blood was trickling from the side of her mouth.

'Lily!' he called. 'Open your eyes. What's the matter, lass?' But she continued leaning forward slowly, so that she would have fallen but for the pull of his hand; and the blood ran on her white collar and down her neck as if it were seeking some hiding place.

His trembling hand tried to brush it away, but more came. So he gathered her up in his arms and set off down the hill, falling over the hummocks, cursing them, cursing the larks which sang so loud and maddeningly round him, cursing the bright, blind sunshine, and the lonely hillside. And presently she was in her house; and after that, she was dead, and he took some flowers to lie near her, and climbed the hill to Slater's End again.

And quite soon, while he was still a boy, he married Maggie Halliday, and now, here he was, his little granddaughter beside him, the years fled away like seeds of grass in the wind. There were his sons and daughters down in the valley, with their sons and daughters; and up here, the old man sat with his dream.

The little girl had tired of the rest, and run away. She had found her way to the rusty gate of the walled graveyard, and was looking through it with interested eyes. She still clutched the cherrywood walking-stick in her hands. The old man's voice came to her from far away, 'Come along, Becky, come along home to dinner.'

'Home to dinner, home to dinner,
There's the bell, there's the bell.
Pudding and potatoes, pudding and potatoes,
Ding, dong, dell. Ding, dong, dell'

she sang, and ran to take hold of her grandfather's hand.

THE APPRENTICE

One warm spring morning a good-looking plumber's assistant of about nineteen came swinging out of a doorway, carrying a porcelain water closet on his shoulder, and whistling 'My love's an arbutus'.

He gave a glance up at the bright blue sky, at the sun in the south-east, and thought with rapture of the evening that was coming, when he would see the young girl, Pattie Lancaster, with whom he had fallen in love. She had promised to meet him, to walk with him. Where could they go? Down Leeds Road, up Apperley Lane, across the fields? No. People would always be passing, and he felt that he wanted to sit down and look at Pattie Lancaster for hours, without any interruption.

Perhaps she would let him hold her hand. He trembled at the idea. Other fellows thought nothing of putting their arms completely round a girl's waist, kissing her, and having their faces slapped soundly for their trouble. But he wasn't that sort of a man, nor was Pattie Lancaster that sort of a girl. She was a star dropped straight from the sky into the grey city. Her hair was yellow, her eyes blue and kind. There was something about her that made him feel as if the whole world was his to conquer. He grasped his burden and trod firmly on the flagged pavement – bing, bang, bing, bang.

His working clothes of blue drill had been washed many times, and shone in all the places where the material was double and the hot iron had gone over it. A small torn place at the knee had curled over on itself. The blue stuff suited him, making his healthy pink face appear even more young than it was. He had dark hair, hidden by a grey cap with a peak pulled to one side and downwards.

Where should they go? The day seemed to be rushing onwards like a dream, and he had not yet thought of a place. Of course, it would be splendid just to walk along the streets with Pattie Lancaster, to look down, adoring her; but there would be more people still – people in desperate, tearing, senseless hurry and scurry, pushing against them. If a man so much as grazed Pattie with his elbow – he grew tense at the thought, his whistling ceased, and an expression of extreme anger crossed his face – 'I'd knock him flying,' he said aloud, staring straight in front of him. A meek little man about to pass him stepped off the pavement into the road, accelerating his pace. The young plumber laughed.

There was Wood Lane, of course. Now that the new road had been made, people had deserted Wood Lane. That wasn't too far. And somewhere near the top, before you got to the newly built houses, there was a gate leading to an old, unused stone quarry. He had been up there several years ago, looking for mushrooms. Two or three tall black trees, which carried only a few green leaves at their extreme tips, had somehow been left standing at the bleak quarry edge. You could see all

the town from there – that is, if you wanted to look at the town.
It might be interesting for Pattie. She could look at the distant
view, and he could look at her.

He smiled ecstatically. How was it possible that everything
had changed in such a short time? All the people seemed to
have altered in some subtle way. Last week he had lived a
different life, had had different ambitions. Wherever his
thoughts ranged now, they always came back to settle round
the head of Pattie Lancaster.

'I love her!' he thought. But he would not dare to tell her so
for years. Would she ever love him? Was she, at this moment,
dreaming as he was, walking through the spring morning on
air?

He was nearing the river, that dark, town river which ran
full and sluggishly under the stone bridge. Today, he thought,
he ought to be walking along the banks of a pleasant country
stream with his beautiful Pattie. They should be going hand
in hand into some flower-filled future. They should . . .

His burden was slipping a little, so the young man rested on
the bridge and began to transfer it from his right shoulder to
his left. Beneath him the light sparkled on the filthy water,
making beauty even of the scum.

As he stood there, he looked with sudden interest and
apprehension up the road beyond. A young girl was walking
down, swinging a market-basket. She had a blue and white
dress on, blue stockings, and low-heeled shoes. He saw that it
was Pattie Lancaster.

She was coming straight towards him, not yet looking his
way. There was nothing he could do, no place in which he

could hide the hideous water closet. He looked about him, but there was only the blue sky, the bare stone bridge, and the river beneath him. He blushed with shame. Pattie Lancaster and this? No, never. He pushed the ghastly white object, which ten minutes ago had seemed only a part of his daily work, into the river. It made a great noise as it hit the water.

The girl looked up and put her hand to her hat-brim. Coming towards her was the young man she liked so much, and with whom she was going out this very evening. Why had her mother made her take this old basket for the vegetables; and why had she put her most childish shoes on? She felt as if she could have sunk through the ground. Didn't he look handsome in his blue drills? As frail as a curl of smoke, the thought passed through her mind that some day she might have his clothes to wash.

'Good morning, Leslie,' she said shyly.

'Good morning.'

He raised his cap awkwardly, seeming to lift his head with it, and they stood looking at each other.

'Did you hear a splash?' she asked. 'I thought I did. I thought perhaps a dog had fallen in the river, or something.'

She was only saying this to make conversation, and wished that she had mentioned the sunshine or the warm air instead.

'No, I didn't,' he answered her politely.

They kept looking at each other and saying they must go. The young man scraped the toe of his boot aimlessly round and round a flaw in the stone paving, and the girl played with a piece of loose straw from the handle of her basket.

'Mother's waiting for some potatoes,' she said apologetically. 'I must be off.'

Yet they did not part, but kept on smiling at each other.

'You won't forget. Tonight at six o'clock?' he said hoarsely, and then blushed at the sound of his own voice.

'I won't forget.'

He turned and began strolling at her side towards the shop in silence.

'Oh, don't come with me,' she admonished him. 'You must go back. Remember, you're working. I only stay at home and help mother.'

The young man went back to the bridge reluctantly, turning every now and then to watch Pattie Lancaster in her blue and white dress and low-heeled shoes. He felt light and free, as if he were absorbing the air and the warmth, and even new life. But when he reached the middle of the bridge he suddenly clapped both hands to his head, and looked with horror over the parapet at the swiftly running river. Then he stood without moving for a long time.

The girl went forward to buy her potatoes, her eyes sparkling, her lips parting in smiles that she could not control. She kept saying under her breath: 'Oh, the poor boy! Whatever will they do to him for that?' For, of course, she had seen him long before he had seen her.

She looked back over her shoulder and saw him standing on the bridge, forlorn. Beneath her laughter a pang of pity shot suddenly through her heart, and, at that minute, she began to love him.

FIVE FOR SILVER

A woman stood on the pavement in Oxford Street one
Saturday afternoon in March, waiting to ask a policeman
something. She carried a baby about a year old in her arms –
a boy, very fair, with serious blue eyes and long, white fingers.
The child was dressed in a blue woollen coat and bonnet. He
was small for his age, and looked rather like a dignified old
man masquerading. Now and again, replying to some intent,
passing glance, he would give a wide, toothless smile, and
then relapse once more into apparent thought. His mother
waited patiently, both arms clasped about him in an ungainly
way. A brown waterproof bag was hanging from her left wrist.

'Can you tell me a nice bus ride, please? But don't send me
to Richmond. I've been there four times.'

She spoke with a north-country accent. As soon as the
words got into his brain properly the policeman smiled,
pulled a bus guide out of his pocket, and murmured to himself:
'Twenty-five, twenty-six.'

'Would you like the East End, do you think?' he asked,
bending to hear what she would say next, ready to catch the
words quickly.

'Oh, yes, please,' she said in an eager, grateful way.

'Well, walk down to that crossing. You see where those buses are coming round that corner ...'

Yes, she saw them, like a great fleet of red galleons bending with the wind and waves, like gorgeous, dressed-up women walking down the steps at the end of a pantomime, like covered wagons dashing across a film prairie. You knew there were only so many, yet they came and came, giving the illusion of something never-ending.

He pointed. 'They come from Victoria Station. They go through the City and the East End. It's a long ride.'

'I've got three hours,' she said anxiously, breathlessly. 'Baby's just been fed, and he wants to go to sleep.'

That did not interest the policeman. He was busy reckoning the times for her. 'You'll do it nicely,' he said. 'Twenty-six is the longer ride.'

'Thank you very much,' she said. The policeman went on giving her directions. She heard him say 'Bond Street' once or twice, but her mind was repeating: 'The City, the East End'.

The bus was covered, and she climbed to the top when a traffic signal shone red, and sat in the front seat of all, putting down her bag and shifting the child on her knee so that he could see out of the window. But he was tired and closed his heavy eyelids. Again she moved him until both were comfortable.

There was intermittent sun and cloud. People shuffled aimlessly along beneath her and the moving traffic raced like splashes of mercury along a board, stopping and staring, it seemed, with no reason.

Her gloves were in the bag beside her. She found it easier and warmer to carry the boy without gloves. There was no wedding-ring on her left hand. Many a time she had been going to buy one for herself, at Woolworth's; or even a gold one, when she had plenty of money. But it was only in shamed seconds that she thought of this.

What hurt most now was that she knew she had made a mistake. The boy's father was not all she had taken him to be – a hero, a god on earth. He was simply a skunk. A skunk who slunk. She laughed, but there was no one else in the bus to hear. It was not a pretty laugh. There was nobody in the bus downstairs either, but the conductor kept calling out the names of streets from force of habit, or for practice, and she heard his voice as if it were a roll of tape, coming upstairs, unwinding itself.

For months, even after he had kept away as soon as he heard her news, she had forgiven him, loved him as passionately as ever, had been infatuated with his memory. His child was to be the most remarkable child – she looked down at the sleeping baby and was pleased with his calm perfection, the regularity of his features, the nobility of his face serene in sleep – a most remarkable child (bound in strong corsets, unloosed with groaning at night, as soon as she had fought that last steep bit of road. 'You are getting wide, Freda.' 'Yes, I know!' She couldn't keep the blush back; but of course nobody could suspect Freda Crowley, never did. 'I eat far too much.' She used to say it frankly, sincerely, smiling).

But that was at home, in the north. And sometimes she stole out, those rain-wet or wind-filled nights of winter, smelling the hidden spring. No corsets then, but a woollen vest wrapped longways. 'I'm taking you for a walk, baby,' she would whisper. And quite foolishly she would go along the road to the edge of the moor where they had been together, alone for the first time.

It was high and quiet, with only the green brow of the hill above. There was a gentle slope into the pastured valley. The night was dark, and very silent, yet they had difficulty in hearing each other's whispered words. She had seduced him urgently, suddenly. He had been angry, and called her vile names. 'What are we to do?' she asked. 'Men don't run after women any longer. And I wanted you.'

He had driven the car back like a madman. A small boy, coming home from the cinema, ran across the road in front.

'Get out of the way, you devil,' he shouted. 'I'll murder you!'

She had felt a little contempt then, but the waves of her emotion had not quite receded, were not to recede for a long time. She was too physically happy. She turned and saw his unhappy face. 'Don't.' Her voice broke. 'Nothing's any different. We're just the same as we were.' He was willing to believe her. He turned towards her, taking his left hand from the wheel, putting it over both of hers, which looked so inert and were so alive (she was without gloves then, too, and the feel of his heavy driving glove made every nerve respond), and murmured something to her which she heard as in a dream through the heavy noise of the car. It was even darker here, on the New Road, than at the moor edge. She strained to see him, the wide eyes she loved, the pale cheeks, the curled mouth with its one-sided smile.

'Now you'll hate me.'

'I'll never hate you.'

Their hands freed mutually, and for a second or two she put hers to her eyes, until she heard him say, 'Don't', in pleading.

For months afterwards she had not seen him alone. When people were there they looked at each other with restless, broken looks, pouring out short, polite speeches like thimble-fuls of brandy.

The second time, he came wanting her against his will. It was early summer. There were smells of cut wet grass and crushed fruit blossom. She would not think of that night. For of course it was night. His for her was not the kind of love that would face the morning light. She could hardly believe that she was in his arms again. He was almost afraid of her quiet calmness. . . . 'And I love somebody else; you know that.'

Yes, she knew that; but underneath, even then, the thought occurred: 'It's a poor kind of love. And to say it now, here with me. He must get a horrible kind of pleasure, saying it. And afterwards, with her, he'll remember me. What'll he say then?'

But she could not help abasing herself before him, saying the words which built up a new picture for himself to himself. He was like an archangel to her, an archangel and a skunk mixed. Not because he had gone away, but because he had gone denying his child in his mind, brushing it out of his mind, forgetting.

She had told him in smiling happiness, expecting nothing. 'Oh, my God!' he said, in terror. 'Can't you do anything?'

'Do anything?' she asked, perplexed. 'What do you mean?'

'To stop it,' he said. She noticed sweat on his forehead. 'What do you think I mean?'

'But I don't want to stop it.'

'If that's how you feel, there's nothing more to be said, is there?'

She saw escape in his eye, and wondered whether to torture him; then decided not. 'I'm going away before long,' she said mildly.

'Look here' (he said 'Look here' quite a lot), 'you won't do anything rash, will you?'

'I won't kill myself for you if that's what you mean,' she said ironically.

He breathed his relief.

'Goodbye. You might tell me one thing before you go.'

She waited for him to say 'What is it?' but he remained silent.

'Have you ever had one loving thought of me?' she asked frankly.

'No,' he answered.

So she turned and walked away to hide the blinding tears of self-pity that came tumbling out of her eyes. He did not follow her.

'Stop it, you fool,' she advised herself, finding her handkerchief with a competent hand.

After the night walks, tied up in the woollen vest, it was harder to squeeze into those gripping corsets in the morning.

She must work, must save money for those few weeks when she would be unable to work. She kept typing bright articles for newspapers on the portable typewriter Uncle Dick had bought for her in the palmy days when he came over from America, quite rich, but not as rich as he pretended to be. For some reason she was able to sell all she wrote, and the idea came to her that she might be able to live in London when her child was born.

Quite early, before the baby had begun to show, she mentioned the idea at home and among her friends and acquaintances. She exaggerated the amount of money she got. With what she would make and what she had saved, she was bound to live. And she had lived.

The bus was now in Holborn. Still there was nobody in it but herself. It felt like a chariot and she like a queen riding it. Memories of Boadicea, she thought idly. It was in Holborn that she had made her first friends. She had been carrying the boy in her arms. He was tiny and delicate, and she would not leave him to another woman's care. She saw a bookshop with the sign BOOKS in blue or green sticking glassily out over the door.

She went in, and there was a bookseller, a big man dressed in blue trousers and a blue shirt with a steel fastener, looking like Jesus, but quarrelling with somebody quietly. She half backed out, but the man said 'Come in. It's all right, we've finished.' He said. 'This is my wife. We were just having a row.'

He threw some books from a bench to the floor, and she sat down quite silent, looking at the bookseller's wife and smiling. Presently she stood up and talked to the wife, whose name was Ruth, and the big man nursed the baby and looked after his customers too.

A man asked, 'This yours, Karel?' and he answered 'No' with an effort, as if he should have been the father of all children. She kept thinking 'I ought to go now,' so she said, 'I can't buy any books. I've got to live on my wits. This baby's mine and I'm not married. But I'm glad to have met you.'

'You come up and spend the day with us on Sunday,' the wife said in her soft, hesitant voice. The bookshop became a kindly cave. On Sunday she enjoyed herself, expanding in warm friendliness. She sat in a cool garden under pale sunshine, and watched the bookseller's children, the blue-eyed, dark-haired one who talked so seriously to a little boy on the other side of the hedge, and the hazel-eyed baby, who wore corduroy trousers and tumbled over every stone on the path.

Before long she was telling Ruth about the child's father. 'It's curious, I despise him, but I still love him. I seem to be marking time just now, waiting for something to happen – waiting to understand why I've done this thing at all. Shall I wake up one day and think I am a sinner? I'm in a fog; I don't understand either faith or repentance.'

'The best thing to do is not to think about it at all,' said Ruth, still soft and gentle. 'Try to make your baby well and strong.' She took him indoors and gave him orange juice.

The City was very quiet, even for Saturday afternoon. The bus rocked and rolled through narrow streets with their vaguely familiar names. At last she was in the Mile End Road. Here was life and colour. The clouds had won against the sun, but fruit stalls cut the gloom, each orange a miniature sun in itself. There were apples and bananas, black and green grapes. Each fruit bloomed with a different lustre, appearing before her eyes, vanishing, and being replaced by a fresh showing.

And here a different people walked. She thought: 'He wouldn't like this road. He would keep away from it (denying it as he denied you, little bastard). He likes the conventional things, tea parties, bridge (with a little cheating thrown in, seeing you're playing for money), Gilbert and Sullivan, my God, shaving cream, hair cut and nails clean, and shoes *never* down at heel; a chapter to finish off the day from a book about the wide-open spaces, or the sea (would he be sick? Would he? perhaps not). "I love somebody else, you know," *that* certainly means church every few Sundays.'

There were Hebrew signs everywhere – black, robust, like the people themselves. In high, injured tones a hoarding whimpered: 'If ye believe in Me, ye shall have everlasting life.' 'What a gift,' she murmured. A young couple came walking on, hand in hand, strangers, gazing at everything with wide eyes, then back at each other, smiling, loving. She smiled down at them, something melting in her heart, and thought: 'That's the first time I've been happy to see lovers for a long, long time.'

The baby slept as if he would never wake again. The bus filled gradually, perhaps because it had begun to rain slightly. The further away it rolled the busier places appeared to be. People were doing their weekend shopping. She was interested, at last, in every one.

As usual the fruit shops were the things she saw most. Calm, placid suburbs with people buying oranges – and every now and then a vile, gruesome murder somewhere. Size nine stockings, and that faint smell of powder on his coat-collar – strange, she hadn't minded it at the time. 'I love somebody else.' She was thinking of his first kiss. The top of a flight of steps with a wooden handrail. Quiet, with dusty sunlight falling gently through roof windows. A speck of that same dust might have been heard falling. She could not remember whether she had shut her eyes or not, but something inside her laughed in triumph at the hard, bitter touch of those heretofore only seen lips. Of course, there is always a first kiss and a last.

The end of the journey came and the baby waked. His face was flushed and drunken with sleep. He stared out of the window, still in his mother's lifted arms, blinking. A horse and van drove up among the houses marked Cloakroom (Who would want to get off here? she wondered), and the boy jumped, smiled, and made some unintelligible noise. A man in uniform came up, changed the sign, and told her that one of the standing buses went before his. 'But we only wait ten minutes; no need to get off.' So she stayed, talking to the child.

The rain came down more steadily now, and the bus filled once more. A woman in black sat next to her, staring out of the blurred window at nothing. She had two talkative children, a boy and a girl of about eight and ten, who stood up, breathing on the window and smearing their arms on it. The baby leaned forward and smiled into the woman's face, but she kept on looking out of the window and would not notice him.

He said his small words to her, and touched her coat-sleeve lightly, but still she stared forward with the same glazed look. They passed a graveyard, the bus stopped, and the boy said in a high, piercing voice, 'My daddy's in there, he's *deaded.*'

So that was it. The woman's husband was dead. Had she loved him? – this tall, angular woman with these ugly, insensitive children. It was like something silly and sentimental in a cinema, the rain, the crowded bus, the boy's raucous voice, the subdued movement of people getting off unwillingly into the downpour.

And the last kiss. 'Freda,' he said it very gently, in surprise. 'I've never called you Freda before.' Neither had he, she had always noticed. But it came with such swift sweetness, he must have thought of her often. She was taken by surprise, and her lips were cold. She did not wish to disappoint him in anything. She thought of his footsteps on the pavement, the glowing light of his cigarette, the hesitation, so faint, so fine, so studied, before he came.

In the hospital where her child was born she had tried not to think of him at all. The nurses had been wonderfully kind. She would not allow his name to appear on the birth-certificate. 'Father unknown,' she had said in a hard voice. Nobody believed her.

She shrugged her shoulders. 'Think no more now, it's all over. Look at these houses, row on row.' But there was a night when baby was ill and began to cry with pain. She sat up in bed saying: 'Hush, darling!' trying to bring herself sufficiently from sleep to light the lamp. When it was lit, the baby still cried with the harsh passion of his pain. She rocked him in her arms, her foot slipping down the smooth sheet. The small, blue-enamelled clock on the table said four o'clock and she was afraid of something she had heard about life being at its lowest ebb at that hour.

He threw himself backward and screamed into the night that was filled with stupor, with remorse, with heavy sleep. She rubbed his little belly, 'Be quiet, my darling, my darling; we'll be sent out of the house, my little one, my own.' But the tears poured out of him, wetting his ears, his hair. She held him passionately, leaning over him, frightened, not knowing what to do. This had never happened to him before.

And she too, had cried, rocking him in her arms. She looked at the empty place in the bed, and thought: '*He* ought to be here. He ought to share this, too.' In a flash of agony she saw him lying, turned away from her, frowning in half-sleep. ('Can't you keep that baby quiet?' petulantly.) She grasped at the dream of complete life between two seconds of time. And when the child was quiet, she lay with him, exhausted, not even bothering to turn out the light, holding the dream like a scroll in her brain and not at all in her arms.

Once she had seen five magpies fly out of a wood. To herself she repeated:

'One for sorrow, two for joy,
Three for a letter, four for a boy.
Five for silver . . .'

'Five for silver,' she thought. 'That's all I've had, not six for gold, nor seven for a secret.'

She was tired, now, and baby was jumping about restlessly, turning, even whimpering sometimes. People still hurried along, hidden under bobbing umbrellas. Rain streamed across the silver-black roads, and the sky hung greyly just above the bus stop. Again she was left alone to go through the deserted City. She began to think of her room with a certain amount of happiness. (Two changes yet, and rain. But people were kind.)

She got off and had a cup of tea in a Lyons shop that was almost empty. 'The world is quite nice today because I have a little money.' She caught sight of herself in a mirror, smiling, contented, ordinary. 'A little longer, and I shall be able to bluff even myself.' But she could not see beyond tomorrow or the next day. Baby would never grow up, she would never change; there would be nothing else definite. She had exhausted herself, tumbling out her treasures all at once like some creature that lays it eggs and dies.

On a table behind a screen she attended to the little one, making him comfortable for the last stages of the journey. 'How did I get here at all? What is there that I have to do?' she wondered, her hands mechanically smoothing and tying. But she had seen fruit in barrows; fruit that made her think of other countries, other worlds, people a little different, who made her think of other countries, too. There was a world forming where there had been darkness so long.

She sat the child up on the table, letting his fingers close round her own. They looked at each other patiently for a little while, then she sighed and said: 'I can't tell you, baby,' and withdrew one hand to feel in her purse for some coppers to pay for the tea.

WHEN WE ARE RICH

A little thin man, with a somewhat shrunken grey suit on, stood waiting at the gate for the hospital to open. A girl of eleven, dressed in a blanket coat, dyed a nondescript blue, stood by his side with a bunch of flowers in her hand.

The day was grey and close, and the flowers in the child's hand shone into the gloom with unnatural brilliance. They were mostly dahlias, scarlet and yellow. The pair looked solemn but gravely happy, as the patient whom they were going to see was now well on the way to recovery. She was the man's wife, and had recently given birth to a son.

'Come on.'

A porter had opened the gate, and the crowd which had gathered moved forward into the courtyard of the hospital.

The little girl, whose name was Sylvia, grasped the back of her father's coat convulsively and moved forward, past the sooty flower beds which now held only grey-green leaves and grass. She had been to the hospital before and knew what to expect. There would be the horrifying cleanliness, the strange, uncomfortable smells, the creakings and movements of heavy women in small beds, the sight of her mother, sitting up and looking strange in a red flannel dressing-jacket, with two greying plaits over her shoulders. And there would be the small, red-faced baby boy, asleep as usual.

The two went in, and the father gave up his card at the office. He was afraid each time that somebody would forget to give him back this card, so he said several times: 'My name is Joseph Emmott.' He then said very seriously to his daughter: 'There's always people ready to keep you out. Come on, come on.' And he pulled her up the steps that led to Ward 5.

Alice Emmott welcomed her husband and daughter by saying, rather louder than she had intended: 'How's Norah's spots?'

The thin, nervous man had become somehow different as soon as he caught sight of his wife.

'Norah's all right, Mother,' he said gently. 'How's yerself, and how's the latest?' He bent over the cot at the bed foot and peered at the softly sleeping child. He was filled with pride because his seventh child was a boy. He had visions of taking him out to fly a kite or sail a boat. The family were very poor, but in his dreams the kite was always a huge, faultless one, the boat better than any toy boat he had yet seen, even in a shop window.

There was one chair near the foot of the bed, and the father carried it awkwardly up to the head and sat down. There was nowhere for the little girl to sit except upon the bed and this was not allowed, so she kept standing first on one foot and then on the other.

The man began to smile widely, showing a lot of big teeth. As he talked to his wife he took on the airs of a big man. He threw one leg across the other, as if it were a great, heavy leg and needed a lot of throwing, and plunged his hands deep into his pockets.

'Well, Mother,' he said heartily, 'things are tip-top at 'ome. Sylvia's doin' champion, and I'm 'olding the fort with the mangle till ma comes back.' He went on in a lower voice: 'I've got that wood for Fred's garridge. I'll make a pot o' money out o' that, see if I don't.'

The woman in bed lifted up her blue-white hands.

'Fred's garridge?' she repeated. ''Is *garridge*? And 'e's not even paid you for the dog kennel yet.'

''E will, 'e will, see if 'e doesn't. As soon as 'e 'as a bit o' spare cash, 'e's promised me. Fred's getting on, you'd be surprised.'

She sighed. 'That wood'll 'ave to be paid for some time.'

'It'll do when I've run the garridge up,' he said confidently.

'Is Mad'line all right?' she asked. Mad'line was the one with the big head and the bow legs. But she had curly black hair so was accounted a pretty child.

'Mad'line's broke a window,' Sylvia said breathlessly. She had been waiting for this moment ever since morning.

'Don't upset your mother, Sylvie,' said the man, frowning. 'Now then, Alice, it's nothing to worry over, I'll soon 'ave that put back.'

'Which winder is it?'

'It's Mrs Torpy's front,' put in Sylvia eagerly.

The baby began to move feebly in its cot.

'Look!' said the father excitedly, changing the subject, ''e *is* goin' to be a strong un!'

'What did Mrs Torpy say?'

'She didn't say anything. Well, 'ardly anything. And if I'd thought you'd no more sense nor talk about it, Sylvie, I'd 'ave left you at 'ome.' He went up to the cot and began to touch the baby's soft head with his forefinger.

'Leave 'im alone, Joseph. You'll 'ave Sister up.'

'What if I do? 'E ain't Sister's kid, is 'e?'

'Go on.' She smiled at him indulgently. 'Sylvie, go to that lady over there by 'erself, Mrs George. She's got twins in that cot.'

'I don't like,' said Sylvia.

'Go on. Do as you're told.'

The little girl went across the ward reluctantly.

'She's doin' really well,' said her father, with a fond look after the child's retreating figure. 'Washes up after every meal and keeps the 'ouse spotless.' This was not the exact truth, but it pleased the woman.

'You're a good 'usband, Joseph, and they're all good girls, though I say it meself. And we've got a little lad at last.'

They both looked silently towards the white cot. There was not much room between the beds, and one or two visitors sat with each patient. Some of the babies – it was a maternity ward – were crying lustily, yet the two parents neither saw nor heard anything but the moving hand of their baby, and the tiny snort he gave every now and again.

The woman thought of Sylvia and Norah, May and Doris, Julia and Madeline. She thought of the small wage her husband got, and of the way he worked at his joinering in the evenings. She thought of how his friends cheated him, never paying for the work he did. He didn't like to dun them, so he put each unpleasant incident out of his mind, and went happily on to the next job. And between them he and Alice managed to pay for the different lots of wood he had bought.

And she glanced from the child to his face.

'Just think, Alice,' he said. 'By the time 'e's seventeen, the lasses'll most likely all 'ave married well-off chaps. I sh'll 'ave made bags o' money. Yes, when we're rich I'll buy 'im a motor bike, see if I don't. 'E shall 'ave a motor bike and go ridin' about like a young swell.'

'We might 'ave a car by then, and 'e might drive us about every weekend,' said Alice, smiling and throwing a thin plait back over her shoulder.

'But there's a lot to go through before that,' she thought silently.

Sylvia came running lightly back.

'Well?' asked her mother.

'They're lovely twins,' said Sylvia. 'Just alike; you can't tell one from the other. I wish we'd got twins, Mother, don't you?' For a minute she had forgotten the extra work that would mean.

The warning bell began to ring, driving them all out.

'Sylvie and Norah'll come to meet you Tuesday, Mother,' said the man, standing up and putting on his cap. 'Let Sylvie carry 'im. And look 'ere, you take the tram. Mind you don't walk. Remember, you've to take the tram. Twopence won't make or break us. Come on, Sylvie.' He walked down the ward, looking round over his shoulder, nodding and mouthing, 'It'll soon be Tuesday.'

'Yes,' she breathed, watching them with wide-open eyes.

'Don't walk. Get a tram.'

PIN'S FEE WIFE

The three sons of the fishmonger Gabitass were dark and queer, and nobody knew them at all well. The fishmonger had a shop in which were sold also hearth-brooms and gramophone records. He sold a good many records, because he always took a penny or two off the price. He would say: 'Well, one-and-three to you, but don't breathe a word of it.' The hearth-brooms were good ones, and hung from the roof in bunches of six.

When Mr Gabitass had been a widower for three weeks he went away and brought back with him what he called 'a young female' to do the housework and help in the shop. The girl, Effie Shepp, was little and fair, with skin and complexion like an early summer flower. She was an orphan, and had been ill-treated a good deal in her life, so that she was rather simple: easily frightened and easily propitiated.

She worked hard from morning to night, scrubbing floors, blackleading ranges, moving furniture about and cleaning behind it. Now and then she was allowed to serve in the shop, and learnt to clean fish. For some reason she liked this. She wore a little green jersey, with the sleeves rolled up, and she would cut up the fish very deftly, talking about it to the customer.

She had no pride, and would say, laughing out loud: 'I'm a servant, I am, and it's a grand place 'ere. My word, if you'd 'ad the life I've 'ad you'd think it was a grand place too. And these lovely records. Look! I can play 'em all day long if I like, when I've washed my 'ands. Mr Gabitass says I can. Can't I, Ronald?' she would call through into the kitchen.

Ronald was the youngest son. He had a long, spotty face and greasy black hair, but he impressed Effie because he used unusual words. He said he would like to be a munition in a ship, and she knew what he meant. He went out with the cart, and had spare time on his hands, so that he often talked to Effie. He would sit in the shop, putting on record after record, and chaffing with her. Once he followed her up to her attic bedroom and tried to open the door, but she was shocked, and called out: 'Ee, you mustn't do that, Ronald. I'll tell Mr Gabitass.' And for a long time afterwards she was frightened, and followed the old man about the house like a forlorn kitten whenever Ronald was in.

Twice a week Ronald would clean himself up, and shave, and put on a white collar and a blue tie with paler blue silk crescents on it, and go to the pictures. He never asked Effie to go with him, and if he saw her outside would turn his head away stiffly. The first time she saw him out of doors she squealed, 'Ee, Ronald,' but he walked hurriedly past her. She was abashed, and thought, ''E *is* grand,' and she respected him much more, even when he smacked her behind rather hard as she passed him in the shop.

The other brothers, Bert and Mitchell, went out to work. Bert was a clerk in the office of a brick works, and Mitchell helped in a garage, and was engaged to the proprietor's daughter. These two were very distant with Effie, and hardly ever spoke to her, though she took her meals with the family. She called them Mr Bert and Mr Mitchell, because they were older than Ronald.

Bert was uneasily ashamed of Effie's presence in the house. He would mumble to his father, 'Can't she eat in the scullery?' But the old man, who had grown fond of the young girl, would not let her go into the scullery to live, as it was very damp and draughty. So she continued with them in the warm, gaslit kitchen, and when Bert brought his friends in he would say, 'Put the tea in the parlour,' without looking at her. Mitchell had his meals in the parlour, too, when his girl came to see him.

Effie could not find any reason for this. 'What's up wi' them? Is there something the matter with their stomachs?' she would ask Ronald, who sat with her in easy familiarity, shirt-neck unbuttoned, legs sprawling over the couch-arm. Old Mr Gabitass would reply: 'Nothing wrong wi' their stomachs, lass, only summat up wi' their brainpans.' It was much more warm and comfortable in the kitchen than in any other room.

Effie was eighteen when the old man died. She was very much upset and cried a good deal, because he had been very kind to her. She helped with the funeral, though that was a niggardly affair. The three sons bargained with the undertaker before they would let him begin. He was a nice, quiet little man called Hackney, and he did not like the way they behaved, as he had never been used to that kind of thing. He took his trade with great seriousness, and could not bear any deviation from what he called the natural rules.

After the father's death, Mitchell married without telling his brothers, collected his belongings, and left. There was only a little money. That went to Mitchell, to help buy a share in the garage. The other boys were to have the shop between them. Never very friendly, they began to hate each other. Ronald could not see why Bert should go out to work and expect a share of the shop takings too. He would sit and grumble to Effie by the hour, and when he had finished he would put his arm about her absent-mindedly, and after a while she ceased to wriggle away from him.

But she was watchful and cautious as well as a little scared. She began to call Bert 'sir', and do little jobs to help him. Bert would not take any notice of her, except to tell her sternly one day that she must in future take her meals in the scullery. He had heard whispers of mild scandal about Effie and Ronald, and would have dismissed the young girl altogether, except that he did not know of anybody else who would work as cheaply and as well.

Effie did not much mind living in the scullery, which was only as cold as the fish. She kept on trying to ingratiate herself with Bert, who remained adamant. When Bert was out Ronald would ask her into the kitchen and either talk to her very grandly or try to take her on his knee.

One night Bert walked in just as he had succeeded. Effie liked Ronald very much indeed, and of late her attempts at repulsing him had not been really strong. 'Why shouldn't I kiss him if I like him?' she had asked herself. So she kissed him very sweetly.

'What's all this, you dirty little slut?' Bert said. He did not shout, but there was a sneer in his voice.

Ronald looked at him with hatred. 'You get out o' here and mind your own business.'

'It is my business. I don't want our family mixing with scum.'

Effie had jumped up and stood looking at Bert, sniffing and biting her fishy hands. She had a red woollen frock on. Her hair had recently been washed. She looked like some pretty, timid child who was afraid of being struck.

All the rage that Ronald had felt for a long time came out. He had given up taking out the cart, and the shop profits were now considerably smaller. An idea of hurting his brother came into his head and stayed there.

'Don't call my young woman scum either,' he roared. 'Me and Effie's courting. Aren't we, Effie?'

'Y-yes,' whispered Effie.

'You're nothing of the sort,' said Bert, glaring at her angrily.

'All right, sir,' said Effie, beginning to cry.

Ronald banged on the couch-end and stood up. 'We are,' he shouted. 'And what's more, we're going to be married at Christmas. Aren't we, Effie?'

This was the first Effie had heard of it, but she dried her eyes and said 'Yes.'

'A fine time to hear of a thing like this when I've just lost my job!' said Bert.

The quarrel ended with supper. Bert had his in the parlour, the other two in the kitchen. Ronald was uproarious, and kept kissing the young girl loudly. He opened the communicating door so that Bert should hear him, but as often as he opened it Bert banged it shut. And Effie's face grew warmer and warmer, and a kind of frightened shame sprang up in her heart as Ronald kept on pawing her with his big fingers.

'Stop it, Ronald,' she begged him. 'It isn't right.'

'Course it is,' he boasted. 'We're going to be married.'

'Yes,' she said doubtfully, 'but "going to be" and "married" isn't the same thing.'

'You're a fool,' he said angrily. 'And I s'll stop bothering with you if you don't mind.'

Now that Bert was at home, Ronald began taking the cart out and regained some of his lost trade. The brothers kept quarrelling about the takings, and sometimes Effie tried to make peace between them. Bert would say, 'Shut up, you,' to her. He had bought some tools and was making a model of a church with all kinds of curious materials: corks, and hairpins, even pieces of chewed chewing gum and tinsel scraps.

Ronald and Effie were married very quietly, and went to the seaside for their honeymoon of three days. It was extremely cold and foggy, and they stayed inside the lodging-house most of the time playing Ludo with the landlady's children. Effie enjoyed this, and would afterwards refer to the seaside as 'a lovely place,' although she had scarcely been outside the house. She could quite believe that fish came from that miserable expanse of winter water, and looked at them with pity when she got back to the shop.

'Poor things,' she would say to the customers. 'Per'aps it's as well they're goin' to be warm for once in a nice 'ot pan.' She felt that now she was Mrs Gabitass she could talk even more to the people who came into the shop. She was perfectly happy, and sang as she went about her work. She loaded the cart for Ronald, fetched and carried for Bert, and on Wednesdays, the afternoon the shop was closed, cleaned in the house.

Ronald still shaved and dressed himself up twice a week and went to the pictures, but he never took Effie with him. He would not take her out at all, so she walked by herself the few minutes she had to spare, and if she passed him just stared at him and waited to see if he would speak. He never did.

Bert kept getting letters with the postmark 'Victoria, Vancouver,' and when he had read them he would pass them across to Ronald. The two brothers had become friendly again, and often left the shop entirely to Effie, going out and not coming back until very late. The customers, who liked the child, would say: 'Aren't you ever lonely, Effie?' but she would reply: 'Ee, no; I've always lots to do.'

Ronald began to grow more and more like Bert. He now looked down on Effie and regretted his marriage very heartily.

'It's this way,' Bert would whisper to him. 'You can't take her about with you. You know, you and me *are* somebody. We've got a shop, and we've a brother who's part-owner of a garage. We could mix with anybody, but just look at her. . . .'

At that moment Effie was pulling the inside out of a fresh herring and saying, a little wistfully: 'I would like a baby.' She was talking to a woman who had a child in her arms. 'But Ronald says whatever should we do with a baby 'ere? There's too much to do. But, all the same, I should like a baby.'

'Just listen to her,' said Bert, nudging his brother and sniggering. 'What can you do with a blabmouth like that?'

Ronald grinned in a sickly way.

The letters from Vancouver kept on coming. They were from a Mrs Lonsdale, a cousin of their dead father. She had two daughters: one called Rita and the other Fay. She kept sending photographs of the girls. One of them was fat and one thin, and, judging by the snapshots, they always seemed to be dressed in light colours and enjoying themselves at a picnic. 'What a life!' thought the two young men. Yet they knew that their aunt kept a boarding-house and that things could not be always like this.

The boarding-house must have paid very well, for in one letter Mrs Lonsdale said that she was coming over, and would most certainly stay with the boys for a week or two.

'I don't know how you are managing since your father passed away (Poor Man),' she wrote, 'but I think you need a Woman about the House. So we are All coming to see you. It will be in May, I think, or early June, just when everything looks so nice in the Old Country.'

'Now what shall we do?' said Bert, in dismay. They had not written of Ronald's marriage. 'Now what shall we do?'

They began to treat Effie more distantly than ever, and once more sent her to have her meals alone in the scullery. On

Wednesday afternoon they sent her out for a long walk. 'Don't hurry back,' said Bert. So she went into the spring sunshine. It was a lovely day, there were young celandines down in the part where a little brook had overflowed its banks. All the trees were bursting into life, and the sky was light blue speckled with white clouds. The young wife went stamping along the road because she had been told to walk, wishing that she had someone to whom she could talk, or a baby to hold in her arms.

'It's been a nice change,' she said humbly to her husband when she entered the house once more. He was reading a green-backed paper, and did not answer her, only shuffled his feet. She took her things upstairs, but the bedroom door was locked. Some instinct took her higher in the house, to her old attic, and there her few possessions were dumped on the bed.

She took the mattress downstairs and aired it, and slept that night alone in her attic. And the two brothers became closer friends than ever, whispering and laughing to each other the whole evening long.

As summer drew nearer they began to do all kinds of housework. They would not let Effie make their meals or wash up after them. For the first time in her life she sat idle, and every time Bert saw her he would say loudly to Ronald: 'You see, she's not much good. We could do without her, quite well.'

She began to mope. 'What's the matter, Ronald? I 'aven't done anything wrong, 'ave I?'

Ronald did not reply.

At the end of May, Bert and Ronald became definitely uneasy. 'They'll be here any day now,' said Bert. 'She'd better go. What do you think?'

'You tell 'er.'

'Sound your aitches, now *they're* coming. You tell her. She's your missus, isn't she?'

'What 'ad I better do?'

'Sound your aitches, you fool.'

'We could send her away for a holiday,' said Ronald.

'That's an idea,' said Bert. 'Send her a long way. To London, say.'

The next morning, Bert said, with unfamiliar jocularity, 'We're sending you to London for a holiday, Effie.'

'Me?' she said, looking up from the range with wet eyes. 'I don't want an 'oliday. I only want to be let go on with my work, same as I always did.' She added, 'sir.'

'You'd better pack your things,' he said briefly. 'All of them. I'll lend you a case.'

''Ave I to?' she asked, looking at Ronald.

'Yes, you'd better,' he said, not looking at her.

So she put all her things into the case that Bert lent her, and the two brothers took her to the station and bought her a ticket. 'Here's two pounds for you,' said Ronald. 'Have a nice time. And don't come back,' he added, very gravely.

'Haven't I to come back?' she said.

'No,' said Bert, 'I shouldn't if I were you.'

'What shall I do, then?' she asked, taking her purse out of her bag and putting the folded notes in it.

'I don't know,' said Ronald.

'Come on,' said Bert, taking his arm. 'We haven't all day to stand here, you know.' He was thinking about Mrs Lonsdale, and Fay and Rita – the fat one and the thin one – wondering if they would have white dresses on and go for picnics in the Old Country, just as they had done in Vancouver. 'Come on, come on,' he said testily.

And the brothers walked up the platform without even shutting the carriage door.

HONEYMOON

They were used to the different bedrooms by now. The first –
that marvellous, soulless, linen-sheeted home – had a
bathroom of the whitest and cleanest next door. 'You go,
darling' (some day, we'll have a bath with silver taps in, she
thought). 'No, you, my darling.' And he would sing in spite of
all the other people; and she would lie on the top of the new
eiderdown, cooling her burning face on the warm pillow,
listening to the tones of his voice and absorbing them.

On the third morning they thought of money. The bill was
surprisingly big, and they were not quite sure about tips.
Downstairs, Bruce left two shillings under a plate, two separate shillings, one for the meek waiter, and one for the
arrogant. But that one had come and stood beside them when
they paid, like a large and stubborn hippopotamus. So the
meek waiter must have taken both the shillings. 'I'm glad,'
Bruce said simply, putting all the change in his pocket.

The second bedroom was in a tiny cottage. Heavenly luck.
It was owned by Mrs Moyce and her sister. There was a long
garden, filled with cabbages and honeysuckle. Mrs Knockton,
at the Floating Light, made their tea, but she didn't want them

for the night. And they had been sent to the Floating Light by a woman miles away, who had flung up her hands to emphasise how scrupulously clean Mrs Knockton was. Mrs Knockton just said, 'I don't mind a *man* now and again, but we're so *busy*, you see, and it's *noisy* in the evenings. Well, if you please, I'd *rather* not, you being a *couple*. But there's Mrs Moyce.'

They whispered and grinned a lot – too much – at Mrs Moyce's, because of a photograph over the bed of an old man with a long white beard and a naughty little twinkle in his eye. And they would linger in the mornings, bathing in cold water and a small slippery china bowl, and Mrs Moyce would shout 'Come, come,' in a warning voice, 'breakfast is cold.'

Breakfast was always cold at Mrs Moyce's; the bacon hard, the boiled eggs tepid. And there were astonishing things on the table, beetroot, and dripping lettuce, and tomatoes as small as nuts. Julie would pass hot tea to Bruce, and when he had put his cup down, pick up his hand and smell it gravely, and think a complete advertisement, because of the carbolic. And she thought of herself, too, at the age of fourteen, scrubbing the front doorstep with the same kind of soap.

In spite of the cold bacon it was lovely at Mrs Moyce's. The woman grew to care for them alarmingly. She brought cups of tea for them at eight o'clock, and hurled her dark blue bosom up the narrow, polished steps each time Bruce slipped down them. 'Be careful, my child, my child. I've warned you, over and over again.' Her timid sister was Miss Lippincott. She had black hair which looked as if it was tied across the top of her head, and she said 'Oh!' in a quiet, unhappy way if the couple came upon her accidentally.

Each day they went out and walked until they could hardly put one foot before another, singing 'Sweet Adeline' in the empty spaces. And however late they got in, there was Mrs Moyce, sitting knitting and listening to a tinny, muffled wireless machine. But she would get up and give them salty ham for supper, and only cold water to drink. And they would wake up with parched mouths at dawn, and creep out for more drinks of water, and look out of the window at the new, dark green hills covered with curls of mist, and listen to the loud, careless voices of the birds.

And she would dreamily and yet with purpose pull her thin nightdress over her head. Somewhere, sometime, it would drop on the floor or on the pillow behind her. She would feel its light silkiness leaving her smooth fingers, and abandon herself without effort to the gulf that was no gulf, but a warm, rushing, upcarrying whirlwind; a wind that would presently leave her spent upon some newer shore; that turned astonishingly into Mrs Moyce's black and brass bed, with Mrs Moyce's deceased and yet so very much alive father musing down from his glass frame; even into the face of Mrs Moyce, and her green lacquer tray with the two cups of tea and the pink glass sugarbowl; and the excited, warning voice of Mrs Moyce, with her 'Eight o'clock, young people', and its undercurrent of 'I know.'

'She's her father's daughter. Perhaps she does.'

Bruce would light a cigarette, and Julie would keep on smiling at him, not having to answer; liking him more and more, knowing that she knew less and less about him each day, but not worrying.

He was clever. So much she had decided in her own mind. But frighteningly aloof. He said very little. Everything he read stayed documented in his mind, ready to be brought out at any time, discussed seriously. She had read hundreds, thousands of books, and they had flowed away from her like seen streams. With an effort, she might recall snatches of them, ripples of rats swimming, trout (always so much smaller than people said), a black waterhen calling to its lone chick. But who should trouble about books, with all the world open before them?

And surprisingly, in the middle of the honeymoon, came an interlude. There was one black flaw in Mrs Moyce's. She had had something sanitary installed in the garden, and you came out of it reeking all over with creosote. They would talk for a long time, enviously, about sweet earth closets they had known, at the ends of long gardens.

'And sitting there, with the door open, watching bees . . .'

'And butterflies, going quietly . . .'

'And bluebottles like businessmen . . .'

'Or very wet rain, and a blackbird jumping out of the apple blossom . . .'

'Or even ours behind the big gate at home, with a taper stuck in a crack of the wood, and spiders to watch.'

So they put their three-and-elevenpenny packs, that were always bursting in strange new places, on their backs again, and said goodbye to Mrs Moyce, full of warmth because her bill was so small. The meek sister had hidden, they feared, in the creosote place, out of shyness; and they rushed away, forgetting to blow a kiss to the old man over the bed, lest Miss Lippincott should suffocate.

They walked into Shaftesbury, and then out of it to find a railway line.

'Let's go on a train, for a change.'

It was thrilling, she thought, not knowing where you were to sleep.

In the afternoon, when the sun was hot and they had walked far enough, they stopped an imposing bus called Greyhound. The fare was a great deal, and she whispered as the conductor made out long, written tickets, 'Why does it cost so much?' and Bruce answered, 'I don't know. Perhaps this is young Alf Greyhound, helping the business on.'

Listening to them, laughing behind them and sucking his pipe, was Blaize Dickinson. Soon the three of them were talking over the roar of the bus.

'Where are you two going?'

'We don't know. Just anywhere. We've booked to Dorchester.'

'Would you like to see my place?'

'Would we?'

They turned to each other, shining-eyed. They had only met Blaize once or twice in London, casually in Charles's bookshop, and had not even bothered to wonder where he lived. This would be lovely.

They climbed out of the bus, and stood like awkward children, waiting for Blaize to tell them which way to go.

'Across the road and down this lane.'

They looked at two clean cottages, waiting to say 'Oh,' and 'How nice,' but there was a long way to go. He took them across a common that was like no common she had ever seen before; smooth turfed, dotted with bramble bushes and sheltering trees. She looked down at the close clover, wondering what was going to happen, leaving the two men to talk because she felt helpless and ignorant.

Bruce had opened suddenly like a flower on a palm tree, meeting another man, one of the kind that Julie called book men. Blaize was carrying a typewriter that he had brought back from his father's. He was going to write seriously at last. But he was young. For two years he had been going to write. Yes, for two years he had lived really in the country, thinking a lot, reading a lot, lazing, gardening, wanting to be left alone, yet with an unsatisfied ache that kept biting at his content. She was perfectly sure that he would write seriously at last, because he had brought his typewriter. All the way across the common she saw genius oozing out of him.

The cottage, when it really came in sight, took their breath away, so that they could hardly say the real 'Oh!' they felt. It stood well back from the lane, at the bottom of a garden of luxuriant vegetation, potatoes and poppies, scarlet runners and sweet peas. It was thatched, and had four windows, now tightly closed. Blaize had been away for a fortnight.

'I don't know what sort of a state it'll be in,' he said. 'We had to rush away for Sally's operation.'

He opened the door with a large key, and they waited in the garden, suddenly shy. Presently he came out with three large, green-mouldy loaves in his arms, shouting, 'I don't know what to do with these. They've made a nasty mark on the tablecloth.'

He had got out of the bus at Salisbury, and bought new Salisbury bread, and butter, and jam. And soon he had a meal ready, and they all ate in love and friendliness.

He said, 'You can stay here if you like for a bit. It's lonely without Sally. I'll be very glad.'

But he could not find the sheets. However, there were some buff curtains, with thinnish bone rings at one end, and a camp bed. Quietly, with complete generosity, he gave up all his own things, the bedding from underneath and above him. But it was summer, and warm.

There was a ukulele hanging in a case from a beam, and Bruce took it down and began playing popular tunes of four or five years ago on it. Julie had not known that he could do this. It made her heart ache to think that for some unknown, youthful reason he had once spent strenuous hours learning to pluck notes from gut with his finger-ends. His face expressed intense concentration. For some time he was not sure of himself, and played badly.

Blaize lifted the instrument out of his hands and sang 'Early One Morning,' as if he had done it very many times before. It was his instrument; he knew it and was used to it. He crowed. But Bruce took it back and afterwards played softly and beautifully, making harmony out of the tinkling strings. The men mellowed and at the same time grew baby-like, and Julie stood aside looking at their wide, momentarily innocent and empty eyes, herself surprised in another whirlwind of wisdom.

For the first time since their marriage they slept in different beds. She went upstairs first, and took the camp bed greedily, because it had the softer mattress. Her head was low, and up near the open window. She blew out the candle, and moved so that she could look into the soft, moist, country darkness. And presently, in spite of the noise from below, the laughter of the men and their deep voices booming through the wooden floor, she slept. Then she woke again. The voices were still going on, but more softly. Outside, the night was still quieter, and she thought that the world was looking up in pain and all the rest of the sky looking down in pity. Imagining perfection, she wept.

When Bruce came up, she relit the candle and watched him undress. He was so serious. All the talk, all the thought, all the laughter had been dismissed coming up the stairs. He took off a sock with a hole in it, looked at it very sadly, told her just where and when he had bought the socks, and how much he had paid for them. Her eyes knew him.

When he was ready for bed, he kneeled down and kissed her good morning. It was almost dawn. She wanted to say to him, 'I don't know anything. I can't talk to you. You'll always have to go to other people for talk. I'm only just beginning to know there are things.' But with his sound, satisfied touch on her shoulder she forgot, and only murmured, 'Go to your bed.' His warm cheek was taken from hers reluctantly. She heard his bed creak, and thought to herself, 'How it creaks, creaks.' And in a minute, it seemed, Blaize was at the door with tea and bread and eggs. He had got up early, and had been to the farm. They could hardly eat for bliss.

His room was filled with books. They ran about the wooden floor with bare feet, pulling a book out here and one there, pushing aside sacks of potatoes and papers spread with onions.

For two days they lived with Blaize chastely, talking, listening, playing shanties and Mozart and spirituals and rather old dance records on the gramophone. Always it seemed to be a mealtime. Blaize did all the work, slowly, so that it did not seem a penance, but a pleasant game.

'Who does the washing?'

'Oh, we do it.'

'That means Sally does it,' she thought. And a new, friendly feeling for Sally grew up in her mind. She had never met Sally, but she would know her, meet her, soon. Would Sally wash the buff curtains, with the white, sewn-on rings? And the pillow-slips, and the towels? Sally would be glad, must be glad for them. She dared not wonder why.

Again on the third day they went.

'You'll come back?'

'Of course we'll come back.'

The next bed was a feather bed. It was the landlady's own, and she gave it up to them. She was big and soft-voiced, and they liked her at once. Julie was happy because they were quite alone again. 'Aren't there a lot of lovely people in the world? Even Miss Lippincott. And Blaize and Sally' (he knew immediately what she meant) 'and now Mrs Wood.'

Bruce kept wanting to say 'How are you, Mrs Wood?'

After the landlady had prepared the feather bed she sent her daughter in with supper. A glass of bitter, a pint of beer ('Thank God for the handle,' Bruce said – he liked his glass to

159

have a handle), some cheese and a huge jar of home-pickled onions. They ate five each, silent with joy. The daughter was a nice girl, big and wide-waisted like her mother. She, too, had a gramophone, and kept putting on her favourite record:

'When are you going to lead me to the altar, Walter,
When are you going to name the happy day?'

The lamps were all on a level with their eyes, so that they stumbled about the unaccustomed passages and tripped up the narrow stairs.

'Shall we go for a little walk?'

'Yes.'

'We'll be in before eleven, Mrs Wood.'

An intense, steel-grey twilight had fallen over the quiet place. The small, decaying town was in a valley, and the downs rose on all sides like truculent shoulders. An incredibly tall, square church tower stood planted, for ever, it seemed, darkening the grey gloom with the shadow that its very age gave out. Except for the occasional sound of a spluttering motor cycle or car on the main road, the night was deeply still.

When the couple had climbed a hill and walked past a grey-walled farm to a new crossroad, they turned back and walked through a small wood, talking in low voices.

She said, 'This can't go on for ever.'

The girl had never known what it was to have a little money. She had always had to work for her living, and this honeymoon seemed to her to be closing as a fortnight's holiday should do.

'Why shouldn't it, darling?'

He was amused.

She could not find words to answer, but she sighed and tried to think of some way of convincing him that life must be taken firmly. That one played for so long, and then worked.

'We've got to find somewhere to live.'

'Of course. Let's take the first empty house we see.'

'What, here?'

'Yes.'

Her heart began to beat quickly. This is what comes of not knowing a man. This is what comes of marrying an income.

'Bruce, have you ever worked?'

'I have. For a whole year. But I didn't like it. And then my grandfather conveniently died.'

Of course, she had known all this, she had asked him these questions before, and he had patiently answered her. But a dreaminess began to grow over her, like the first beginnings of moss on a stone wall. There are people who don't have to fight for every penny. Now I am one of them. I didn't realise it. In the same moment she hated and loved the stranger by her side, and feared the thing she could not realise.

'You're not worrying, are you? You know there's enough for two of us to live on.'

'Of course I'm not. But you don't earn it. It'll be a different kind of money from any I've known. Listen to the trees.'

There was no wind at all, everything around was still, yet, high up, a small, murmuring leaf-noise could be heard.

'They're talking to us. Must be. There's nobody else about.' She could see the gleam of his teeth through the warm darkness, and for some reason began faintly to tremble, to look for glimpses of dark sky through the tree-tops, to escape from thought.

'My sweet, my love!'

When they reached the inn it was late, and Julie felt guilty because of the warm and shining happiness which had routed thought and left only a bemused desire for sleep. 'Mrs Wood won't mind,' Bruce said, exerting himself enough to sprint down the last stretch of straight road. 'And we shall be in bed in five minutes.'

There had been a car breakdown, and the inn was still brightly lit. For Mrs Wood had recently installed a petrol pump. She hovered about the car which would not go, full of goodwill and the knowledge of her petrol.

They said good night and closed their door behind them. Bruce lit a candle, and they examined their new room for the first time. It was full of presents from Weymouth, from Bournemouth, and from Poole. A small windmill had Marken on it. There were shell-sided boxes with glass-topped views, and wooden boxes with Weymouths and Bournemouths and Pooles on them in pokerwork. Bruce lifted a lid gingerly, and found a collection of childish handkerchiefs and coral necklaces and bracelets and other presents from Weymouth and Bournemouth and Poole. There was a large, framed photograph of a solemn, black-moustached man with letters an inch high beneath it, 'A Happy New Year From . . .'

'Marken must have a history all to itself.'

The night was warm, and the bed was warm, too, but they slept close and unmoving until after ten. Everything was leisurely. They ate in a tiny kitchen, and then had sandwiches packed, and walked over the downs all day long. There was a wind, and some light, thin showers. They walked for long stretches without speaking, dull under a dull sky. Grey-striped flies stung their arms, and each time they sat down to rest or eat, small, unknown insects bit their legs.

Julie was near tears. She had come upon a gap in the crowded days. Besides, all the rest of the times there had been sunshine. 'Does he feel like this, I wonder?' she asked herself.

She longed for her home, her mother and sisters, even her brothers. Bruce was alone, but for her, without mother or father, brother or sister, uncle or aunt. He was used to being alone. She forced back her tears and sat silently scratching herself. Bruce was finishing a sandwich at her side. She looked at his great dark head, his wide, fanatical brown eyes, his large-nostrilled nose, his eyebrows like chips of jet, his lips that looked hard and were surprisingly soft, and the thin but very definite line of his jaw, and wondered why she had once thought of him as 'that quiet boy', and had recalled his presence with an effort. 'Yes, you come, Bruce. Come with us,' and of how he had started willingly forward, just as he would have stayed willingly behind. And yet, all this had happened. His quietness that was as sure as anything on earth is sure. His certainty and her mercurial nature together. The things he thought, and the things she thought! Yet occasionally they were the same.

That night they talked for a long time. They could not sleep. She lay high on the pillow, her hand under his arm, his head on the satiny plain of her breast. The clouds had drifted away with the sunset, and a silver, almost full, moon was rising, dimming their yellow and still-burning candle.

All their talk was foolish talk; snatches of past days. Now and then they hurt each other, trying to sting as the flies had stung them throughout the day. Under their backs the feather bed grew warmer and warmer.

'Let's go out.'

'How dare we?'

'What do you mean, "How dare we?" Who's to stop us?'

'Well, I mean, how do we get out and back?'

He was already half-dressed. 'Through the door, of course.'

She had to beat back the words from her lips, as she realised she would always have to beat them back and follow the man silently.

She put on her clothes. There was the responsibility of leaving the inn door open. Why didn't Bruce think it was important? There was the fact that if they were not back by early morning Mrs Wood would think the strangest things.

'Quietly.'

Before he blew out the candle flame he looked over his shoulder and laughed. She laughed and took his hand, and they crept downstairs together, their blood in perfect rhythm. The house was very old, and creaked and groaned in its troubled sleep. The air was chill outside. For a time, past all the houses, they walked on tiptoe.

'Where are we going?' She looked up at his face, pale and austere and once again inexplicably dear in the moonlight. They were now walking on a white lane between two hedges.

'We're going to see the giant in the moonlight.'

On the hillside in front of them was a great figure cut from the chalky ground. Upheld in his right hand was a huge club. His face looked small and round and far-away.

'We're going to climb to the top of the hill.'

'Yes,' she said contentedly.

But it was hard to find the way, and she feared the treacherous moonlight. 'Bulls, bulls,' she kept thinking; and she saw illustrations in magazines of enormous, snorting bulls running after people who had no earthly chance of escaping from them. Bruce walked in front of her, looking for some kind of a track, and she plodded behind him, conscious of every hillock, of every bush or stone that might move and prove itself to be a bull. But gradually something in the cool and moonlit night took hold of her and overcame her fear.

They were almost breathless from rapid, purposeful movement when at last they reached the face of the giant. They looked at what could be seen of the sleeping village on their left, the dark trees, the square tower of the church which now seemed to be no longer Christian, but sheer pagan.

'Come here.'

She came willingly, and sat down with her husband on a raised nostril of the friendly giant. First the hill seemed large to her, then the country, and the sea surrounding it. She thought of high hills, of Alps and Himalayas and Andes, and then again of this place where two humans sat under the moon; this hill not more filled with secrets than any other hill, but holding evidence of other lives that had been lived here long before them.

She sat for a long time, near her husband and yet apart, looking into the night silently. But first her small vexations had to go: the open inn door, the candle-grease that Bruce had spilt on the pillow, her own vague longing for home and the life she had formerly known.

She felt peace inside herself at last. Had she been brought here to learn of this gracious silence from the night? To accept life as this hill accepted time? For how many thousand years had the man-carved giant shaken his defiant club at the sky? Nobody knew. Tomorrow he might be gone, broken in bits by some freak volcanic upheaval, even sunk to the bottom of the sea. It did not matter. Some new man would make some new wonder on some new hill.

She wanted to break a piece from this enchanted night and send it down the ages; but there was nothing to take. There was only the thought of the down that billowed around them, the darkly silvered trees in the valley, the shut and sheltered houses, the solemn ecstasy of the moonlight, the ebb and flow of the near and distant sea; and that thought would go on.

Within an hour they were back at the inn again, and asleep. Their faces were calm, smooth, and unshadowed. And at that instant not even Time himself could have guessed with what lines they would be engraved when he had finished with them.

FOR A SMALL MOMENT

The two little boys hesitated for a moment, not sure that this was Mrs Taybrow's gate. What a long garden, what a lot of flowers and trees! Their own garden, sooty and dirty, lay nearer town, and was more a cat haunt than anything else. They had a swing in a sunless corner near the garage, upon which Vince swung Alan, and Alan swung Vince; there was no swing in Mrs Taybrow's garden, but it was so bright, so sunny, so clean!

Come in, come in!' called a voice from the door. They were relieved. There stood Mrs Taybrow, and she knew them. She wore a long, stiff kind of black dress, with a starched white apron over it. Her brown hair, faintly streaked with silver, was drawn back from her brow, plaited in a soft-looking plait, coiled, and pinned at the back with big, brown tortoiseshell pins. She was smiling kindly, but her large hazel eyes looked sad all the same.

The boys walked up the path. They had such thin, bony white knees, such blue-veined hands and temples, that Mrs Taybrow's eyes looked sadder than ever

'Miriam,' she called to somebody upstairs, 'the children have come.'

The girl Miriam come dashing down the stairs and was at the door as soon as the boys. She had been watching for them out of the window. 'Hullo,' she said, 'would you like to go for Cousin Louise straight away?' She was a year or two older than Vince, being eleven. She radiated a tense sort of excitement, her dark eyes flashed, and she kept showing her teeth in quick smiles. She couldn't help jumping first on one foot, then on the other, as if she were skipping.

'Yes, please,' said Vincent politely.

'Well, come on, then.' She took hold of their hands, swung them round, and ran down the path. The boys began to smile. Everything had been so miserable at their house for a long time. Each morning – excepting last week when they had stayed at Aunt Margaret's house – they had had to go into 'mother's room', that dull room with grey wallpaper and light brown curtains, and say 'good morning' solemnly to the thin, unhappy figure in the dark, wooden bed. 'There must have been a time when mother was downstairs, when she got washed and dressed, and took us out for walks,' Vince thought; but he had almost forgotten it.

Cousin Louise lived not far away. She was ready and waiting to be fetched. She was a pretty child, with fair hair in ringlets and a round, pink face. Miriam felt proud to be walking with Cousin Louise, and even with Vince and Alan, though she did not as a rule care much for boys.

'Look here,' she said importantly, 'I'm going to be the mother today. I've thought of lots of things to do.' She was to be left in charge of the house for the first time, from ten in the morning until four. There was to be a cold lunch for the children, and it was laid ready in the kitchen, scrambled egg sandwiches and tomatoes, and jam which she herself had helped to make.

'Oh, let me be the mother,' said Cousin Louise, halting as if she would go back unless her request was granted.

They all stopped on the dusty road. A bantam cock called hoarsely from a farm across the field, and a faint wind rustled the leaves in the hedge. The boys did nothing. They were dressed in blue serge suits which did not fit them very well, and their hands hung loosely by their sides. Miriam looked at them critically.

'All right,' she said. And Cousin Louise walked ahead, saying, 'Come along, darlings,' in a silly, mincing kind of way.

Mrs Taybrow was standing by the gate, all ready to go out, when the party came in sight.

'Hurry up,' she said impatiently, 'I shall be late.' A wasp was flying about her head, and she kept flapping at it spasmodically with a black-bordered handkerchief.

Miriam felt suddenly full of responsibility as she saw her mother with her hat and coat on. What could she possibly do with the three children all day? Cousin Louise was going to be no help, only an added care.

'Look after everything,' said Mrs Taybrow. 'I've tied the back gate, so no hawkers'll come.' She looked in a kindly way at the two grave-eyed boys, and bent suddenly and kissed them. They both said, 'Thank you,' and did not rub their hands over their cheeks. She hurried down the road with tears in her eyes.

As soon as her mother was out of sight, Miriam began to jump about madly. 'Hurray,' she shouted, 'we can do what we like. We can go up into the attics and down into the cellars. Come on, let's play follow-my-leader.' She led them on a mad chase all over the house, convinced that this was the best way to entertain her guests. Released from all restraint, the children screamed with laughter at her antics, and Alan shouted, 'Bullabaloo' in a surprisingly loud voice. Soon they were all shouting, 'Bullabaloo'.

'Did you make it up?' Miriam asked, and, without waiting for an answer, said, 'come on downstairs now and let's eat everything.'

It was not yet half-past ten, but they ran noisily into the kitchen and began snatching at the things on the table. Miriam hopped about the floor with a sandwich in each hand, and Vince blew down into his glass of milk. He made such loud, bubbling noises that they all tried to do it, and blew the milk out of the glasses on to the floor and even the walls.

When they had finished, they sat down breathless for a while. 'What shall we do now?' asked Cousin Louise. She had come in a clean muslin frock, but she had slipped in the coals during the game of follow-my-leader, and soiled it a little.

'Well, there are some gooseberries in the garden, but we haven't to touch them.'

So they went into the garden and ate a few gooseberries, and for a long time played hide-and-seek. For some reason, the boys were very good at this. They had much patience, and found good places to hide and stayed there. Miriam and Louise were always wanting the game to go on, and jumped out if the seeker came anywhere near them.

In a surprisingly short time it was afternoon. The two boys had changed entirely. They had become rowdy, noisy, full of spirits which matched Miriam's own. Only Cousin Louise looked on disapprovingly now and again. 'You'll catch it when your mother comes home, Miriam,' she kept saying, ominously.

'I don't care,' Miriam would answer, a reckless light burning in her eyes, and you don't care, do you. Vince 'n' Alan?'

'No!' they kept bawling.

'Do you know how to make toffee?' Miriam asked suddenly.

'You don't make toffee; you buy it in shops,' Alan said. Not that *he* bought it; he had never had any spending money. His father was stern and severe with his two boys.

'Well, I can make it,' Miriam said. She had once helped, that was all, but was certain that she could make toffee if she tried.

'Get mother's cookery book out of the front table drawer,' she ordered, 'the recipe's in there. We'll do it properly.'

'"One, two, I wouldn't be you",' chanted Cousin Louise. She had long ago realized that there was to be no mother-play with these boys, no nice, quiet games of 'house' and 'school'. In some way, Miriam had spoilt them. They looked as if they had always been so dull, so good. They even admitted they had never played like this before. But now they had red faces and dirty knees, and kept going off into cackles of laughter, just like babies.

The boys flew to the pantry for butter, and to the cupboard for demerara sugar, tumbling over each other, fighting for the packets. 'Put these towels round you so you don't get dirty,' sang out Miriam, 'we're going to do this properly.'

She lit the gas stove carefully, followed all the directions in mother's cookery book, and turned out two small tins of lovely toffee.

'Don't touch it; it has to cool, to set,' she cried out fearfully. But her disciples revolted. They got spoons out of the spoon-drawer and ate the toffee soft, drawing hardening strings of it up to their mouths and chins.

In the middle of all the mess, there was a heavy footstep. Miriam glanced at the clock, guiltily. It was four, and her mother was back. Really, they had meant to tidy everything up, to have the rooms nice and straight again. She looked round almost with fear. This was certain to mean a smacking, though she *was* eleven.

But Mrs Taybrow did not look angry. She called the two boys to her side and put her arms around them. 'Are you having a nice time?' she asked.

'Oh, yes, a lovely time, a lovely time,' they stammered eagerly. 'Miriam's made some toffee; will you have a bit?'

'No, not now,' she answered, taking off her black hat. 'We'll have tea, and I'll take you back home. Put the kettle on, Miriam.'

She seemed subdued, unlike herself. Her eyelids were red, as if she had been in tears at some time of the day.

'Mother,' said Miriam in sudden loud astonishment, 'have you been to a funeral?'

'Hush,' said Mrs Taybrow. 'Why, where's all the butter gone?'

'You know, mother, it's in the toffee. Whose funeral was it?'

'Now we shall have to be careful with butter for the rest of the week,' said Mrs Taybrow. But she did not seem to be annoyed. She was mechanically putting things straight, talking now and then to Cousin Louise or the two smiling boys.

'We played hide-'n'-seek, and I got up into the poplar tree and Cousin Louise couldn't find me for hours,' said Vince.

'Yes, 'n' I went behind the big gate, and Miriam couldn't find me, either. I am hungry,' said Alan simply; 'we ate everything as soon as you'd gone.'

They were glad to sit down to tea and have brown bread-and-butter, and stewed fruit and custard. This was a way of enjoyment, too, and Mrs Taybrow was so kind.

'I wish mother could get up and make tea and play with us,' said Vince, slowly putting down his piece of bitten bread. 'I'm going up to tell her what a lovely day we've had the minute I get home. Do you know, it's nearly a week since we've seen her. We've been staying at Aunt Margaret's,' he explained to Cousin Louise.

He picked up his bread again and began to laugh at the thought of the toffee: '*I'll* make some when I get home,' he vowed.

Mrs Taybrow washed Alan's hands and face, and let Vince wash his own. Then she put on her hat and coat again and took the little boys home. They could have found the way by themselves, but she wanted to deliver them safely into their father's hands. She wanted to say to him, 'Let them come over whenever they can. The fresh air will do them good.' It was all she knew how to say.

Their house looked, somehow, darker and sootier than ever, the earth of the garden more greasy. Their father was waiting in the hall, and he said 'Good afternoon' to Mrs Taybrow in rather a surprised sort of way. It was not long since he had bidden her farewell.

'I've brought the boys back, Mr Mcleod,' she said, 'and I want you to know that they'll be welcome at our house any time they care to come.'

'Have you been good boys?' asked their father, bending down sternly and without the shadow of a smile.

'Oh, father,' said Alan, 'we've had such a happy day, the happiest I can ever remember!' His face in that dark house was lit with pleasure.

Vince had slipped his hand out of Mrs Taybrow's grasp and was quietly climbing the stairs. 'I'll go and tell mother about our happy day,' he thought.

But when he got into that cheerless room with the grey walls and the light-brown curtains, it was empty. There was the bed, with a clean white counterpane over it – but it was quite, quite empty.

MISS CREECH OF REDEMOUTH

Thelma Creech lived with her thin and aging aunt in a small coastal town. She was twenty-seven, and though good-looking, of medium height and build, and possessing a soft, low voice, she had few powers of attraction. She used to long, at times, for an understanding woman friend. Men she met. She talked to them, played tennis or bridge with them, and occasionally dined or danced with them in a simple black frock that had a disappearing flower on one shoulder. But to her they were all glass walls. She knew simply nothing about men; but she thought a lot.

One rather cold and windy day in May, before the season had properly opened, she was taking her aunt's dog for a run along the promenade and thinking that every young woman of twenty-seven lived with her aunt and took undying dogs for eternal runs. She was dressed in a long fawn coat with a scarf and a small cap of the same colour.

The beach at Redemouth was filled with round, bluish-grey pebbles of varying size. There was very little sand, so that the town was used mainly as a health resort for elderly people, and children were rarely seen. This day the high, grey sky, the loneliness, the green and yet discouraging look of the cliffs filled with new spring grass, the breathing of the dog, the wind flapping coldly in the skirts of her coat, got more than a little on Miss Creech's nerves. She frowned as she walked, and wondered if there was nothing she could do to vary the monotony.

In the green-painted shelter where the cliff started, she saw a man reading what looked to her like a schoolboys' weekly. He was about thirty, with a strong red face and light brown eyes. She took in every detail of his appearance, because it always pleased her to notice people.

To begin with, he had a hard straw hat on, and she took an instant dislike to that. She thought, if he must wear it, why not do so on a sunny day. Yet that was no business of hers at all. He had a thick new tweed coat on and creased flannels and a blue shirt. She did not like his shoes, which were of canvas and leather mixed, in white and brown. Also, he was a short-kneed man, which meant that though he looked tall sitting down, he would not do so standing up.

Suddenly, he laughed at something he was reading, and Miss Creech thought how extraordinarily good-looking he was. At the same moment he glanced up at her, still grinning. Without quite knowing what she was doing, the young woman sat down at the other end of the shelter and smiled back at him.

'Funny how these kids' books come back and get you, isn't it?' he said sheepishly.

'I beg your pardon?'

She sat there, looking at him composedly. She had heard what he had said, but did not know what to reply. Her eyes roamed over him. He raised his hat, which was stuck to his forehead somewhat. She still kept on looking at him, and he replaced the hat uneasily. He winked at her, rather mournfully. In a minute she had hidden her face in her hands and was laughing uncontrollably. The man laughed too, and the fat dog barked, and some gulls swooped down, mewing.

Then Miss Creech got up, pulled the dog after her, and hurried off up the promenade. The man watched her for a while, thinking 'rum bitch', and then philosophically returned to his paper. He re-crossed his legs, feeling chilly, turned up the collar of his new tweed coat, and tapped his hat down firmly. When he had read for five minutes, he heard a noise, and saw that the girl with the dog was coming back.

Miss Creech had decided that something must be done. She did not know how to get on with the men she knew, so she would practise on an unknown man. In spite of his funny clothes, he was handsome when he smiled. She had felt as if she were ready to burst, and her aunt did not take kindly to her tempers. Yes, she would talk to this man, she would make herself attractive. She would look at him, flatter him, really get to know him; find out something – anything, about men from him. Why should she keep on feeling like this, all dog and aunt. It wasn't fair. As well make a start here as anywhere.

She sat down again. Then she said in her nice, low voice, 'I never read a book like that. May I look at it?'

'Certainly.'

After three days, which kept on being cold and windy, Miss Creech had seen a lot of Bob Fearon. He had asked her to call him Bob, and sometimes in the night she said to herself, 'Oh

Bob, Bob, Bob, Bob, Bob,' as if she were counting sheep; yet it sounded silly. And she felt that she knew less and less and less about men. The two of them had been to see a film, they had walked over the cliffs alone, they had taken the dog for several runs, they had talked about life; but for all that, everything was just where it had been three days ago.

The fourth day opened fine and warm. Miss Creech woke in her incredibly tidy blue room. There were her clothes, folded neatly, just ready to put on; clean stockings rolled for her waggling toes. She slept quietly, without tossing. The bed-clothes had scarcely stirred. The window was open two inches at the top. Everything was as it should be.

And for breakfast she had a softly boiled egg and one piece of toast; then a second piece with a little marmalade. She had put on a pale green linen frock. Her aunt always had breakfast in bed, and she took that up and had a second cup of coffee, sitting in the prim bedroom chair. She admired her aunt, because she was like herself, and she felt that she might grow old in the same way, with a dog and a rather competent maid, and perhaps a niece to – to smother.

'I'm going out for the whole day, Aunt Gina,' she said softly.

Her aunt said 'Oh?' in an astonished, questioning way.

'Yes, I'm going to take a long walk. I feel rather restless.'

'Oh,' said her aunt, in a different way this time.

'And I'd rather not take Punch, if you don't mind.'

'Oh,' said her aunt, with still another intonation.

'Today, everything is going to be different,' said Thelma to herself. She felt quite a new woman. And she looked nice. The constant smiles of the last few days had improved the look of her face. She had brushed her brown hair until it shone. Her cheeks were thin and rather pale, but her fringe prevented her face from looking too long.

She carried a light coat with her as she went to meet Bob Fearon. You never knew, the weather might be treacherous – and she caught cold easily. The man was waiting for her in the shelter, reading a paper gloomily – the very same one he had been reading when she first met him, she thought. She looked at him coolly. He was without hat, he had on a plain fawn shirt, and had bought a pair of ordinary buff sandshoes. All due to her nice, playful little hints, she thought. But his face was uneasy, he looked almost dim. She did not see that.

As they walked along the cliff edge, Miss Creech took his arm. It hung lifeless, but she kept squeezing it with her fingers. The morning was still early; it was not more than ten o'clock. The sun shone warmly, and there was only a breath of wind as they reached a hollow of the downs.

'Shall we sit and talk?'

'All right.'

He sat stiffly, while the young woman draped her coat and sank down on it. 'You don't often sprain your ankle, do you?' he asked.

Miss Creech thought that this was a strange remark to make after being silent so long. 'Oh, no,' she answered, smiling at him ardently, 'I've never done so yet.'

'I'm glad of that,' he said simply.

She looked down at him pensively and yet possessively. Bob Fearon was troubled. He had never been looked at in that

way before, and he did not like it. Talking to a girl was all right
– he had talked to girls for ten years without any harmful
result – but there was something about this that he did not
like.

'Why don't you tell me more about yourself?' she said, in
what she thought was a most seductive way.

'I've told you all that's interesting,' he answered.

'Yes, all the things that don't matter. But yourself, yourself?
You've told me you keep hens as a hobby, that you have been in
an aeroplane once, that you like bread-and-butter pudding.
But that isn't what I want to know. I'm thinking more of your
immortal soul.' She glowed, thinking that she was getting on
very well indeed, until she saw his face. Suddenly she said,
'Smile for me'.

He did not want to smile, and looked out to sea.

'There's a boat,' he said.

'Never mind the boat. Look at me,' said Miss Creech.

He looked, and saw a thin face with small, lightish eyes,
the end of a brown fringe, a straight nose, narrow lips, a
pointed chin with a spot of some kind on it.

'Let's walk on,' he said; 'I don't like this place. Besides,
what's the use of sitting down. We're not tired, are we?'

'Very well,' she said, brightly and nicely.

It was no use. She did not know the way to make anybody
interested or interesting. She had gone out of her way to do
something for, or get something from, this man, and here was
the same blank wall. She did not know why. The same kind of
thing had happened before, and would probably happen
again. But she would not be resigned. Anger and resentment

began to burn inside her. Why should she go on like this, being polite? But her voice said sweetly, 'Let's walk down to the beach.'

There was another small town at the foot of this down. It was just a shade livelier than Redemouth. There were more shops, and more cars flashing along the white roads. They could see the main square, in which a few buses stood.

'We'll have an ice, shall we?' She still kept on talking brightly.

They had an ice, and then went to sit on a kind of wooden jetty. There were no railings to it, but here and there deck chairs had been placed in pairs. It was warm and pleasant in the sun. They sat at the far end, isolated, listening to the murmur of the sea not so far beneath them.

Here they sat silent for a long time. Then the girl stood up and yawned.

'Can you swim?' she asked, in a voice a little louder than she generally used.

'Eh?' asked the man, just awakened from a nap. 'Can I swim? Yes, I've done quite a lot. At the Baths, you know. I can do four lengths without any bother.'

His chair was at the extreme edge of the jetty. Bending down, the girl made a quick movement, seized hold of the wooden part in her strong hands, and in a second had tipped man and chair into the sea.

All the splashing and gurgling and shouting she heard quite well as she walked slowly and sadly down the jetty towards the little town. One minute she felt that she had gained some knowledge or experience. Another, she thought,

'No, it is in the past, and there has been nothing gained at all.'
There was some knowledge, but she would never be able to
make use of it.

SALEM STREET

Lawrence Shaw and his wife Nellie rarely went out together, except sometimes on Saturday afternoons to the quack market. They had not been married many years, and once, all their clothes must have been new. But they, and their house, and even a brown-and-black dog which they owned, looked mildewed. The black part of the dog shone faintly green. They had no children.

The man was a packer, and though he brought his wages home every Friday night, and even kept accurate accounts as to the way they were spent, he never managed to save any money. The two of them spent hours studying catch advertisements, and cast odd shillings, occasionally pounds, into some scheme which never bore one sickly blossom, let alone fruit.

Their house was in a very long road called Salem Street. All their furniture had been bought in salerooms, and often, to get the cheap thing they wanted, they had to buy a great deal of rubbish – huge, chipped, china ladles, rusty weights and scales, even in one lot eight mahogany table legs – and when they had got what they didn't want, they kept it in corners, or under the bed, as if they couldn't bear to part with a single thing. There were times when Nellie would stand staring at them, a greyish yellow duster in her hand, 'wondering' as she said, 'where to begin on them'. Then she would hear the milkman or grocer; or something else would attract her attention; and she would trail away to the door, forgetting the dust altogether.

The couple were very much alike, with mid-brown hair and light-brown eyes. They talked in low tones to each other, and never quarrelled. Yet there had once been romance in their life.

Nellie, whose name was Helena, was the daughter of a rich businessman who rode to town each day in a horse carriage. He kept the blinds down, and also had cottonwool in his ears so that he could neither see nor hear the motor cars which roared past him. In the same way he politely kept progress from the doors of his business, having neither a typewriter nor a telephone in the place. Yet so solid was the concern that he managed to make money and to leave it, not to his daughter nor his son, but to a missionary society.

Even before he died, Nellie had met Lawrence Shaw several times. He worked in the packing cellar, below the warehouse of her father's place, and was sometimes sent up to the boss's house on some errand or other. He spoke quietly and pleasantly. She often thought of the young man when he had gone.

Nellie had not a great deal to do. The house was not so large. It was detached, and stood in the middle of a stunted garden. It was sooty, because it had been built on the east side of the town, and the prevailing wind came from the west. But old Tunnicliffe had always been used to the east, and would not change. Rows and rows of grey streets now compassed the ugly house. In one of these, Lawrence Shaw had lived. He was not used to women. Nellie was not used to men. They met in a shop one day. He walked home with her, by a devious route – round by the west of the town, where High Park Lane was. Along High Park Lane, with its lovely, solid houses and comfortably treed gardens. It was spring. Light rain was falling. There were many lilac trees in bloom on High Park Lane, and all the evening was coloured mauve and grey. They never forgot their first walk.

'Miss Tunnicliffe?'

'Yes, Mr Shaw.'

'It's very good of you to let me see you home, Miss Tunnicliffe.'

She did not answer, only walked along quietly smiling into the gloom.

'Miss Tunnicliffe?'

'Yes, Mr Shaw.'

'May I see you again some time Miss Tunnicliffe?'

'Yes, Mr Shaw.'

They clasped each other's hands.

At that time, Nellie looked well after her father and brother, cooking a large midday dinner for them and a more simple meal at night. In spite of the old man's money, they kept no maid, but an elderly woman came each day to help with the housework and the washing.

The old man was small and square-faced. He wore a squarish grey hat, and was always dressed in grey. He had a watchchain made entirely of his late wife's hair; yet he had not liked his late wife at all, and was quite relieved when she died – that is, happier after the funeral was over and his daughter Helena had stopped weeping.

The brother was a peculiar man. He was tall and cadaverous. He never believed anything he was told, and was always trying to verify facts. By long and involved processes he had proved so far that everything was a lie, that nobody ever told the truth. Sometimes he said, holding his hand in front of his mouth as if he hated to let a word escape from him, 'You have only to look at clocks. Never two of them alike. If they look alike, they're some fraction of a second different.' As nobody he knew could prove anything to the contrary, he was thought to be a clever man. He had wormed some money out of his father and become, after long years, an accountant. But Helena had never thought to worm anything, so she was left quite unprovided for.

She did not mind, for by the time her father was buried, and all the family affairs were settled, she and Lawrence Shaw had got married at a register office, and without the vestige of a honeymoon – unless attending salerooms was a shadow of a holiday – had gone to live at four hundred and two, Salem Street.

One day Lawrence brought a book home from the public library which had a good deal in it about personality. He read most of it up to his wife, sitting uncomfortably on a hard, wooden chair with a still harder cushion under him. Nellie was knitting. She often started knitting things with grey or fawn wool, looking at directions in the free pamphlet given with the wool. But always something went wrong, so that she rarely got an article finished. She would go on repeating the directions, and had once made a sleeve a yard long, going helplessly on from the book, feeling that it was not right, but not knowing where until she reached the very end.

She sat listening, yawning now and then, and passing a knitting needle through her hair. She was wondering how soon they might go to bed. She liked sleep. Each night, about ten, she would open the door to let out the dog, wind up the alarm clock, undress hurriedly down to her long, 'natural' coloured vest, in which she always slept, slip on a sleeved and collared white nightdress, say 'Come on' to her husband, and wait impatiently for him to turn out the light. Often he had to go downstairs again to let in the whining dog. Then Nellie slept until the alarm clock woke her.

'There's a lot of information in this book, Nell.' He kept looking up from his book in order to say things.

'Is there?' she asked, thinking of nothing, except her knitting, and her eyes, the lids of which sometimes twitched.

'We haven't much go about us, have we?'

'How do you mean?' she asked, but without much curiosity.

'Well, we don't know anybody. We haven't any friends, particularly. We don't get about, do we! Look at your Ernest. He's an accountant. That's something, you know. We ought to go and see him, some time. He's your brother, isn't he? He's got a house, and a wife and family, too. We're an uncle and aunt, aren't we? There's a lot in this book about making the most of your opportunities in life which' – he sought for a page – '"passes us like a song that is sung, its echoes lingering but for a moment on the – the pregnant air, and is gone".'

Nellie thought it over for a moment.

'Ernest never troubled himself about me, and I never did like him much. I know Mrs Freer, and Mrs Catlow, and Miss Warman. We're all right as we are.'

But Lawrence could not get his new ideas out of his head. Somewhere in his greyness a small spark flickered. He kept the book beyond the regulation fortnight – it was non-fiction, entitled to an extra week – and read it two or three times. He began thinking recklessly. Could he even get a better job? Something might come of a visit to Nellie's brother. After all, Ernest lived in a smart house, was on the telephone, and his offices in town were quite large and well known. He and Nellie had attended the wedding, though they had never seen Ernest since.

So one Saturday in early spring they set off to call on Ernest. It reminded them of their earliest walk, though the lilac was not yet in bloom. But the evening wore the same colouring of grey and mauve. Herton Hill stood up against the place where the sunset should have been, with the two small churches and the large mill thrown on the skyline. The couple plunged into the gloom of Park Crescent and began looking for number twenty-five.

The house was already black and solid-looking, though Ernest had had it built at the time of his marriage. It stood some way down a gravelled drive, and had a kind of con- servatory at the entrance, which was, however, quite empty. The door, as well as the wood surrounding the panes of glass, was painted white. There were long curtains at the long house windows.

At their ring, a small, solemn and very fancily-aproned young maid opened the door. She could not have been more than fifteen years old. The pair were rather taken aback, and did not quite know what to do. They had expected Ernest himself, or his wife. Even one of the children. But not a servant.

'Is Mr Tunnicliffe in?' asked Lawrence.

'Yes.' The small child stood staring at them, one hand on the door knob.

'He's my brother,' said Nellie. 'We want to see him.'

The little maid was not quite sure how to act. She invited them into the glassed entrance, and scurried away down a wide hall. They stood silent, in the middle of another surprised silence, and soon Ernest came.

He had not altered much. Beside Lawrence, he looked taller and more cadaverous than ever. He half smiled, and immediately covered the smile with his hand, as though it might admit something.

'Well, Helena, this is a surprise,' he said. 'What brings you here?'

He led the way to a very small and very cold room. There was an electric radiator standing in the hearth, but he did not switch it on, though he looked at it hesitantly once.

'Sit down.'

They sat, awkwardly, looking at him. Then Lawrence dropped his gaze to the small, fringed carpet and looked at that instead, and wished he were back at home. Nellie frowned and coughed.

'We thought we'd just come along and see you,' she said in a low voice.

'Yes?'

Lawrence could think of nothing. Not one word would come out of his dry mouth. The book had taken him to the door, but not over the step.

After a long silence, Nellie rose and began to walk uncertainly round the small room, looking at the pictures on the walls, at the curtains of the one window, at the electric radiator.

'Well, we just thought we'd like to see you,' she said again, without smiling. 'Come on, Lawrence.'

'That's right,' said Ernest, 'come along again some time.' He had not taken the slightest notice of his brother-in-law. He swung away from a small oak table, against which he had been leaning, and led the way from the room back to the entrance. Then he shook hands with each of them, solemnly, and said good night.

The pair walked back to the garden gate, down Park Crescent, and so to the main road, without speaking. Here it was lively. Lights were appearing everywhere, and the busy Saturday night shops were sparkling in the twilight. A fat, smiling couple were just looking at some pork chops held out to them by a fat, smiling butcher. A cat was slinking along under a fishmonger's slab with something in its mouth. Four people met in the middle of the pavement and blocked the way unconcernedly.

Lights appeared, too, in the gaudy, leaded windows of a public-house bar.

'Nellie.'

'Yes?'

'Let's go in here and have a drink of something.'

'Oo, *no*, Lawrence.'

Neither of them had ever been inside one of these places.

'Come along,' he said stubbornly, taking her by the arm and drawing her through the swing-door. 'Anybody can go in. I'm going.'

She followed, blinking at the strong light, the strangeness, the barman – who seemed to her to stare curiously – the queer, pump-like things from which she guessed beer was drawn, and the rows of different coloured bottles. There were two or three round, solid tables. She sank down on a chair near one of these. Her husband stood beside her, breathing fairly quickly, watching her nervously opening and shutting her handbag.

What shall we have? A glass of port wine each?' he asked.

Nellie nodded her head speechlessly.

Lawrence went up to the bar. 'Two glasses of port wine,' he said angrily.

'Small or large?' asked the man indifferently.

'Large,' said Lawrence confusedly. 'No; wait a minute. One small and one large.' The barman seemed already to have poured them. 'All right, all right,' Lawrence muttered dismally. The price was high, he thought.

He carried the glasses carefully across to Nellie. Then they gulped the drinks hastily down, as if they were obnoxious medicines. There were times when they had drunk port before, but they were not many. For a while they sat at the table, feeling slightly unreal. Then Nellie said, very slowly and distinctly, 'I think I should like another glass of port wine.'

'So should I,' said Lawrence. He stood up abruptly, walked to the bar with his empty glasses, and said 'Fill these again'.

The barman looked at him with a flicker of interest, got out two clean glasses, and filled them from the same bottle. Lawrence carried them back less steadily, frowning with concentration.

'I'm sorry, Nell, I've spilt a bit.'

Nellie looked up at him, laughing. 'Never mind,' she said, waving her hand airily, 'never mind.'

She drank in sips this time, smiling at her husband and looking at him even roguishly now and then. He unbuttoned his raincoat and spread his legs, staring at his boots as if he had never seen them before.

'My word, Nellie,' he said suddenly, 'but I *have* big feet.'

She laughed with uncontrollable mirth, as if he had said something exceedingly funny.

Then they both began to think of their visit, and of Ernest. They became grave. Lawrence leaned over.

'We ought to have asked after Florence and the children. Yes, we ought. It was rude of us not to ask about Florence and the children. I think so, don't you?'

Nellie was silent. Then she said, uneasily, 'Yes, I do. And don't you remember, this was going to lead to something? You were going to ask Ernest if he knew of a better job. Why,' she began to laugh again, quite loudly, 'we simply forgot all we went for. Let's go back!'

'I don't know about that.' Lawrence pondered as though it were a question of State. 'I'm not sure that Ernest was really pleased to see us.'

'Nonsense!' Nellie shook her finger at him playfully. Her greenish-black hat had slipped back from her brow, and her face was flushed and almost bright. 'He shook hands warmly – quite warmly. And he partic-lary-lary said we'd to come along again some time. Let's s'prise him.'

The bar was full now. She had to raise her voice to be heard in the din. Lawrence was startled. 'Yes, Ernest is my brother, and Florence is my sister-in-law. We ought to have made full inquiries. We were not even polite,' she kept on shouting. 'We must go back immediately.'

'Very well, Helena,' said her husband, with a kind of dignified quietness.

Night had fallen when they got outside again. The cold air made Nellie sway a little, and she took Lawrence's arm, and went on talking. She had nothing to talk about except her knitting, her dog, her house, Mrs Freer, Mrs Catlow, and Miss Warman. And Lawrence talked, too; about his work, his boots, his opinion of Ernest and his house. 'A nice fellow. Quite a nice fellow. But not very easy to get on with, perhaps.'

Nellie would not have that. 'I ought to know. He's very clever, and quite easy to get on with. I never had any trouble with him. He was never any trouble at all,' she said tranquilly.

They walked along very slowly, until the fumes from the unaccustomed wine dissolved and rose like little mists away from their heads. Night had come without stars. There were reflections from street lamps, yellow on the wet-looking pavements, and occasionally a pale-green young leaf gleamed wetly, too. They had left the main road, and were wandering once more in the quietness of Park Crescent.

When they rang the bell of Ernest's house this time no little maid appeared. A light was switched on, and Ernest himself came to the door. He peered out at them with astonishment. Lawrence's raincoat was still wide open, showing his shabby suit, and above his waistcoat a little of the crumpled front he wore in place of a shirt. Nellie's hat was still on the back of her head. She clung to her husband's arm. The world seemed a nice, peaceful place to her. She spoke warmly and yet dreamily.

'I'm glad to see you, Ernest.'

Ernest looked at them closely, coldly.

'Yes,' he said, closing his lips with a snap, and turning their corners down. He looked more cadaverous than ever as he turned his head sideways, so that he might hear any sound from the house. 'Have you forgotten something?'

'We forgot to ask how Florence is. How is she?'

'Very well.'

'And the children?'

'Very well.'

'Oh.' They stood uneasily on the stone step, blinking at the bright light in front of them. Lawrence cleared his throat.

'Do you know of . . .' he started. 'Do you happen to know of a job that might do for me? Something better than my present employment. Something in the nature of . . .'

'No, I don't,' said Ernest, softly, his head cocked still more to one side in an effort to hear something at the other end of the hall.

194

'You've got a nice house, Ernest, a really nice house,' said Nellie, still as warmly and dreamily. She sighed, and let her head fall on her husband's shoulder. She felt very, very sleepy.

Lawrence was not sleepy. He felt alert. He had forgotten the exact nature of the job he wanted. He was thinking, too, of the nice house that Ernest had got. He would like very much to ask him if he was going to fill the bare-looking conservatory with plants some day, but words would not come. And suddenly the light went out, the door was closed, and the couple were left outside, in the cold spring darkness.

Nellie lifted her head from her husband's shoulder.

'Has he gone?' she asked, without much interest.

'Yes,' Lawrence said. He kept on looking at the white-painted door. 'That was rude.'

'Well, let's go home, then.'

'Yes, but all the same, that was very rude. I wouldn't have done it,' he said, but without anger.

They walked to their well-known house again. The greenish-brown dog welcomed them silently. Lawrence gently poked the fire until it lit up. His head was beginning to ache.

When Nellie had taken off her outdoor things she picked up her knitting with the free instruction book, and yawned. She, too, felt that her head would soon ache. She looked at the clock. Oh, dear, hardly half-past eight. An hour and a half before she could wind up the clock – not setting the alarm because it was Sunday in the morning – undress before the fire, and go to bed.

Lawrence Shaw sat in the hard chair for a while watching very small flames jump up, coal redden and fall away to grey ash. Then he took a pencil out of his pocket and a folded paper from beneath the cushion, and began to work afresh at one of his competitions. His tongue stuck out, and occasionally he wetted his pencil point with it and wrote words along the margin of the journal. Presently he called to his wife.

'What do you think of this, Nell? I'll read you the example first. Listen. It's Riches. See? Riches. Well, I've put "Wee want, we want" after it. The first one's spelt with a double "e". "Riches", "Wee want, we want". I might get a thousand pounds for that. It sounds like a real winner to me that does. What do *you* think, Nell?'

THE WHITE LINE

The little girl stood at the door with her pink cotton night-dress done up in a brown-paper parcel. She was hungry, ready to eat at an eating time, and sleep at a sleeping time, but nobody appeared to be expecting her.

Last Sunday, Lily had said, 'Oh, Phyllis must come up and meet our little Ivy. Can she come next weekend, and stay Saturday night? I'll bring her back here again on Sunday.'

Her mother had said 'Yes,' politely and rather drearily, and all week long, Phyllis had thought about little Ivy, magnifying her into a kind of angel. But by the weekend everybody seemed to have forgotten. Saturday morning turned into afternoon. She ate her dinner and stood about, stiff and miserable; and of a sudden burst into tears and shouted in an anguished, accusing voice, 'They said I could go to see little Ivy for the weekend, and Lily would bring me back on Sunday.' She went on crying until she was nearly sick. All the directions were jumbled in her mind. She was to take two tramcars, and Lily would meet her at the corner of Wash Road at four o'clock.

It had all come right. She had had her face washed again, and Andrew had taken her to the first tram, full of troubled instructions.

'Now, Phyllis, be a good girl, because Lily is going to be your sister some day. I want you to let her see how nice you can be.' But there was a dark, worried shadow on his face.

Phyllis could feel that Andrew was not in the least happy. She knew when he was happy, though he was over twice her age. When he was playing cricket with the so-carefully-chosen team; looking tall and slim and nice in his flannels; talking to Lou or Carmen Isles, who loved him, Phyllis thought, almost as much as she did herself. When he was setting off for a long walk with Noel Sharpe, his shorts flapping above his knees, the golden hairs on his calf gleaming. She could look up, then, and see his white, uneven teeth showing themselves in smiles, hear his shouts and laughter as Noel called some incomprehensible thing to him. But not since he had known Lily.

He was just walking along with his little sister now, his steps slow, a frown between his brows, his eyes dull. He answered her absently, and she grieved in silence.

She didn't say 'I will be good.' It wasn't necessary. She had never been away alone before, even for a night, so of course she would have to be good. There was nothing else to do.

This was a funny door, flat to the street. It had a glass panel that said J P Elms, and underneath that, Painter and Decorator in fancy letters – so fancy that it took her a long time to read them. She stood there so long, after her first knock, with the nightdress parcel clutched tightly and yet almost slipping from her arm, that she read them several times.

Then the door opened and somebody came out dressed in street clothes, a little, plump grown-up with lovely red hair, dressed wide and waved under a wide hat.

'What do you want? Do get out of the way,' said the girl crossly. She had been crying, too, Phyllis saw, and her eyes were so puffed that they were almost closed.

'I've come to see little Ivy,' Phyllis said.

'Then go round to the back.'

She smoothed down her coat, looked about her defiantly, and went away down the street.

Phyllis had no idea where or what 'the back' was, but in the end, a little boy took her down a side street, through a wooden gate, and left her near the open door of a scullery. Loud, angry noises were coming out of the house, and she could not help hearing Lily say in a voice so different from any she had ever heard before, 'She's a slut, a disgrace to the family, and I for one won't speak to her any more. Spoiling my chances, that's what she is, the dirty cat. I've known for a long time what was going on, but I thought she'd enough sense to keep herself out of trouble.'

'Lily, Lily,' came a whining, trembling voice. 'Be sure what you're talking about, be sure it's true. She hasn't said anything, you know.'

'Hasn't she? Anybody with half an eye can see it now,' Lily's voice shot back. 'A fine bridesmaid she'll make at my wedding, won't she, with her belly stuck out half a mile? There goes the bride, I don't think. Just wait till dad comes back. I'll tell him, and see what she has to say then. He'll belt her, and serve her right.'

'Don't tell dad, Lily,' went on the pleading voice. 'He'll half kill her. And we don't want any trouble or any hitch about your wedding. We'll all have to keep it dark till afterwards.'

'I will tell him – I will!' Lily's voice was loud and shrill. 'She must take what's coming to her. Why, only the other day she was making sheep's-eyes at *my* Andy, and her like that. I'll teach her. People'll be saying it's his, if I'm not careful.'

'Do be kind, Lily. Glad's only eighteen, only a child yet.'

'Only a child,' Lily repeated, 'but she's old enough to make fools of every one of us. I've kept myself to myself for twenty-two years, and the first time I get a decent chance she has to go and mess things up for me. Where's she gone now?' She paused, but there was no reply. 'And we're going to get to know who it is. Yes, I'll tell dad all right. I've said I won't speak to her again, and I won't. Wild horses won't drag a word out of me. But dad'll make her tell, and if it's a married man – but that's her lookout. She should have thought of that before.'

Phyllis knocked, and an uneasy silence fell. Nobody came for a few moments. Then Lily appeared, smiling, one hand patting her hair.

'Oh, goodness gracious,' she said in an artificial voice, 'it's *Phyllis*, ma. Whatever made you come to the back door? Oh, oh!' She slapped her brow with her hand. 'It's all my fault; I'd forgotten. I asked you to come and see little Ivy, didn't I? Come on in.'

She dragged the child through the scullery into a small,

hot kitchen where a wizened but not old woman was sitting shelling peas.

Phyllis felt that she ought to say something, but no words would come to her. Lily went on, 'You don't mind, ma, do you? I asked Andrew's little sister to come and stay the night. She can sleep with Ivy. Is that your nightie, Phyl?' she asked playfully.

'Yes,' said the child. The wizened mother frowned and went on shelling peas. 'It's all the same to me, Lil, but you might have told me. Ivy's bed's none so big, and with all this bother coming on us . . .'

'Well, I don't mind a bit of inconvenience, and I'll put off telling dad till tomorrow. But look here, I'm not sleeping with her any more. I'll sleep with Ivy tonight, and Phyllis can go with Glad. *I* don't mind a bit of inconvenience,' she said again.

Phyllis stood there awkwardly, feeling that she ought to be polite and say that she would go straight back home. But she could not. All the week long she had been living in dreams of this visit, and she could not bear to spoil it. She felt she could have listened for ever at the door to the strange Lily who was shouting about something and saying she would tell dad. And who was this Glad with whom she had to sleep ? She had had visions of sleeping with little Ivy in an exquisite white bed. She wanted to love Ivy as she loved her brother Andrew and nobody else, not even mother and father. And she knew that Glad would be the plump and crying girl who had left by the front door as she came.

'Would you like to come upstairs?'

Lily stayed behind as Phyllis mounted the steep wooden stairs near the front door, and spoke in a rapid whisper to her mother. The child stood at the top of the stairs, holding her parcel and sniffing. The windows were closed, and everything smelt of new, strong varnish. At the bottom of the steps the fancy blue and pink letters of Painter and Decorator were wrong way round. There were three doors, all closed.

When Lily came up, she took her first into a large room at the front. It was carpeted all over, warm and close, and there were three mirrors and a very large, high bed.

'This is ma's and dad's room,' she said.

Phyllis was stunned. For a minute she had thought that she was to sleep in this magnificent place. All her life she would remember that bedroom with its dozen pictures, its score of ornaments, little china boots and bowls on the mantelpiece, the glass things on the top of its dressing table, its red and green and yellow carpet. Her own home seemed to her a very poor affair after this.

The second door belonged to little Ivy's room, which was a third-rate edition of the big room. It was packed with things, but was small and dark. The third door opened on to a flight of steps, which led to an attic.

'Here's my room,' said Lily gaily. 'Well, mine and Glad's, really. But you can sleep in this bed tonight. Put your parcel down.'

The little girl, still speechless, was looking at the clean walls and sloping ceiling. There was a patchwork cover on the bed, and she immediately loved it. And there was a picture above the mantel of the girl she had seen at the door; but in it the girl was smiling and pleasant and pretty. She had a wider, kindlier face than Lily.

'Is this Glad?'

'Yes.' Lily's tone was short. 'Is this all you've brought? What about a Sunday frock?'

'This is my Sunday frock. I've got it on. I didn't think I'd need anything else.' She didn't want to explain to Lily that everybody at home had forgotten, just as everybody at this end had forgotten, too, the visit she had so much longed for.

'Where is little Ivy?'

'Oh, she's playing out somewhere,' said Lily carelessly. 'You can go and look for her. Only don't get lost.'

She wanted to tell Lily that she had never met little Ivy, but by the time she had really thought of it, Lily had let her out by the front door.

'She'll be about somewhere. Come in to your tea soon if you can't find her.'

The afternoon was warm, but Phyllis had taken her coat off in Glad's attic. She had a dark green velvet frock with a swing pocket, and a straw hat with daisies and a maize-coloured ribbon on it. She stood for a long time twirling the string of her pocket round her finger, and letting it untwirl itself. There were some other children playing farther up the road, so she drifted towards them and watched.

Presently she caught a ball and threw it back to them, and soon she had joined in the game, still without speaking. She played all the time without speaking, making cries in imitation of the others. It was quite pleasant.

There was a small, rather ugly girl with thin hair dribbling down her back in tails, who kept putting her hand in her pocket and taking out a sweet and eating it without offering the bag to the others. Everyone called her Ivy, and Phyllis was afraid she was the Ivy for whom she was looking. This Ivy stopped a man to ask him the time, and then ran down the road, shouting 'It's teatime' to the others. Phyllis followed her, and ran around the street corner to the back door again.

Ivy turned indignantly, 'Hey, you can't come here. This is my house.'

Phyllis stood stock still on the step, and would have stayed there all evening had not Lily come out and taken her by the hand. 'Now you two, don't quarrel,' she said in the same sweet, artificial voice she had used before.

And soon they had all settled down, and were eating ham and salad, and drinking tea from cups with yellow flowers on them.

Dad had come in. He was a big man who sat in shirt-sleeves and sweated in the kitchen heat. Blue sweat stains on his blue shirt spread from armpit to elbow. He had a wide mouth and mutton-chop whiskers. Phyllis admired him, and thought how much better he suited the bedroom than little wizened ma.

He had a special couple of boiled eggs to himself. Phyllis could hardly eat for watching him. He was in a good humour, and talked to her. Lily and ma and Ivy watched him, too, but as if they were waiting to jump up and do things for him, rather than to enjoy him as she was doing. He had a round white mug with a coloured border. Lily refilled it three times for him. And he ate more than she had ever seen eaten at one time before.

After tea, she went out again with Ivy and played until darkness fell. Then they went back to the empty house. She could hardly keep her eyes open, but Ivy had to stay up to wait for the others. Mrs Elms had gone out long ago. Dad had taken himself off immediately after tea, and Lily had got ready soon after him to go to the theatre with Andrew.

She had let Phyllis watch her dress. Lily had done so much to herself. When her face was first washed she looked even uglier than little Ivy, but by and by things began to appear. She did so many things that Phyllis was fascinated. She made her skin, her lips, her eyebrows look different. She seemed to know each strand of hair, and to torture it into position. When she had finished, she was not at all like the shouting Lily of the kitchen.

Phyllis thought suddenly, 'This is the only Lily Andrew knows.' A lot of things seemed to grow clear to her, but she forgot them, playing snakes and ladders.

When it was very late, and she could hardly prop her eyelids open, Ivy said, 'Let's go and watch the pubs come out. I do it every Saturday night. Once a drunk fell in right through our front window. It's lovely watching them.'

So they went out and sat on the cool step. The night was very dark and glowing faintly with starlight. There was no moon. The air was fresher than in the kitchen, and Phyllis waked. She sat clasping her knees and looking up at the sky, thinking lovely things, remembering holidays on the sands when Andrew had played cricket with her and let her bat all the time; and when he had taken her into the sun-warmed sea and helped to teach her to swim; when they had walked too far, and he had said, 'You're only a baby yet,' and had picked her up and carried her along interminable roads until they were home again.

'You haven't got much to say,' said Ivy disparagingly. 'I've even seen a drunken woman fall in the gutter, and you never laughed a bit. I don't believe you're looking.'

But Phyllis was drunken with sleep herself and could not see.

'Look out, our Glad's coming.'

All that Phyllis recollected was the whole family walking in at once, with the exception of dad; and Glad saying to Lily, 'It might interest you to know that I'll be married before you are,' and of Lily turning to her mother and saying with contempt, 'She's a dirty liar. And she needn't think I'll ever speak to her again,' and flouncing off to Ivy's room.

Then the visitor was helped upstairs, each step feeling a mile away from the last. Kindly fingers helped her off with her clothes and helped her into the soft, patchwork-covered bed. And soon she was sound asleep.

She awoke with the first dawn light. Sparrows were shouting 'chip, chip,' monotonously under the near eaves. The bed was moving softly because Glad was shaken with crying.

She lay blinking for a minute, and then remembered yesterday, and all the things she had heard in it. She put out a hand and touched Glad. 'Don't cry,' she whispered.

Glad made no change; she only went on with her dreary sobbing.

'Please don't cry,' she whispered again. She did not know what else to say, so she slid her arm under Glad's neck, and leaned over and kissed the girl's hot, swollen face.

'Get off. Leave me alone,' said the girl fiercely.

She lay without moving, listening to the noise of the sparrows. Cold tears began to creep from under her own eyelids.

'I'm frightened,' she whimpered.

'Oh, shut up and go to sleep. You go to sleep while you can,' Glad said. 'Soon enough you'll be sorry you were ever born.'

The child's fingers were caught in the girl's soft hair.

'You have got lovely hair,' she said reverently, stroking it. 'Lovely, lovely hair.'

'That's what he said,' Glad muttered. 'Once.' She broke into fresh sobs. 'Leave my hair alone. Go to sleep.'

'I can't. I want my mother.'

Glad opened her swollen eyelids. 'Shut up. Do you want to waken the whole house? All right, well come here then.'

She put her arms gently round the child, and began to sing to her as if she were very small indeed:

'Oh, hush thee, my baby, thy sire was a knight,
Thy mother a lady, so gentle and bright.'

'That's nice,' said Phyllis gratefully, 'and you have got lovely hair. You're good and Lily's wicked.' She went off to sleep again while Glad was singing,

'And all this fair . . .'

and did not wake again until Ivy came running over the floor and jumped on the patchwork quilt.

On the way downstairs they peeped into Ivy's room to look at Lily. Her face looked small and mean on the pillow. Glad, with her tears, had her own soft skin and hair, and it was nice to lie beside her. There was something wrong with Lily.

The child went home on Sunday afternoon. Lily had put her brown-paper parcel into a leather bag, and was carrying it for her. Lily was dressed very neatly in a dark green costume. She had some cream lace on, and something cream-coloured interwoven in her hat. Her hair was pulled from its confining pins and tortured into a hundred curls. Now and again her lips grew tight and straight as she thought of the coming interview with dad, of the bitter things she would say about Glad.

Andrew met them, but his little sister could not smile for him.

'Have you had a good time?' he asked perfunctorily, looking all the time at Lily.

'Yes, thank you,' she answered unheeded.

'Well, run along, Phyllis. I'll look after Lily.'

He put his arm about the girl, but she shook it off, coquettishly. 'Don't, Andy, you know I don't like to be touched.'

'Can I take your arm, then?'

'No, why should you?'

Phyllis took the leather case with the nightdress in it, and went with dragging steps to her own room. She looked at the muslin curtains blowing in the wind, at her white counterpane, at the doll she called Felice lying crookedly across the little white chair she had used as a baby. Her heart felt heavy.

During the afternoon, when Lily was talking to her mother, and Andrew was alone in the garden, she went out and stood beside him.

'I don't like Lily.'

'Oh?' He looked at his sister moodily, then across to his mother, whose sleek head he could just see. Lily was standing there, too, and she smiled and blew him a pouting, inviting kiss, secretly. Her lips shaped the words 'Come on.'

'Andrew!' The little girl grabbed her brother's hand. 'Don't go to Lily, I don't like her. She's bad. She's bad!'

But Andrew merely pushed the child aside angrily, and she watched him walk across the lawn as though he were a bird, and a chalk line had been drawn between himself and Lily.

AFTERWORD I

When I saw downs for the first time they were familiar to me because of a cricket field I frequented at the age of four. This was only a small field. The pitch was in a hollow, and a grassy bank rolled gently up from it, to be crowned at the summit by a couple of eastward-bowing sycamore trees.

It was under one of these trees that I composed my first poem, ran home intoxicated across the cricket pitch, through a game in progress, stammered it breathlessly to my father, was given sixpence, and spent it, all within an hour. And almost thirty years later the same thing repeated itself in a more dignified fashion, with an editor in place of a father.

I live now within a few yards of that cricket field. The trees are cut down. A road runs through part of it, but I can still see it in its young-century beauty, feel the early summer warmth, know again the glory of the sun and the daisy that provoked the poem; because at that very moment (I could already read and write, being the eighth of a family of eleven) I became aware that I was in a marvellous place, that I was alive, and that I must say so.

My second poem was not so good. What I really wanted was another sixpence. I repeated my poem, which had given me a lot of trouble, but my father merely said, 'You're too late, lass. Shakespeare said this first, and much better,' and kept his hand in his pocket. So I went and pulled out a loose tooth – we got a penny for things like that – and thought a lot.

Afterwards, when I wrote anything, I would look at it for a long time, grow certain that somebody else had done it better, and tear it up. Anyhow, reading was so much pleasanter. I learned how to be deliberately naughty (I got noise of the ear-splitting kind into a fine art) so that I could be sent to bed where I could read in ecstasy, alone, and not have to look after one or more of my three little brothers.

Luckily for me my father was a bookbinder, so there were always plenty of books. Sometimes people would leave books at his place to bind, and forget to return for them. They were put in an attic, and so was I. It is hard to remember the names of all of them. There was *David Copperfield* – though for many years I never got beyond page forty of him – *Wuthering Heights*, volume after volume of the *Family Herald Supplement*, *Tom Jones, Peregrine Pickle*, bound copies of *Tit-Bits, All the Year Round*, and *Today, Les Misérables* (how I ploughed through that one), Andersen's *Fairy Tales, Vanity Fair*, and an old Bible.

The ones I could not read were *Don Quixote* and *Jessica's First Prayer*. There was a *Child's Bible* which I tried, but did not find suitable after the real one. I would look for words like hell and devil in the real Bible, and simply go on reading because I liked the rolling sound of the sentences. At my first school I got every Scripture prize going. There was also a book called

Little Meg's Children, which delighted me at an early age. In that, or another very much like it, there were the words 'Perseverance, paint, and glue, Eighteen hundred and eighty-two.' I thought it a better poem than any of mine. And I was right.

At my second school I was a nasty child. I hated it so much, and was so miserable that I was forced to make a world of my own to get along at all. There was a three-mile walk to it, and that I enjoyed, summer and winter. There was so much to see, so much to do and think about. One of my favourite pursuits was following streams. If they went underground, so did I. But all I got was cold and dirty; I got torn clothes and smackings, too; and atmosphere.

There were no prizes, and no good marks of any kind for me at this school. I did my worst work at examinations, not from nervousness, but from contempt. And the whole of the time I was steadily writing and burning everything I wrote. Only once did I betray myself. We were told to write a story, and mine was read in front of the class. Feeble as it was, it was apparently the best of the lot. I was in an agony of shame. I remember telling the other girls that I had copied it out of a book. Somebody told the form-mistress, and she kept me behind and asked me why I was such a liar. I don't know what I said. All I wanted to do was get away.

About that time I read a story about a child who formed his letters so crookedly that one night they came out of the book, dragging themselves lamely in front of him, wanting to be made straight. That is what my own sentences still do. For a long time after my first book was published I used to wake in the night while badly expressed and broken paragraphs crept in chains of horror before my eyes. But I am trying to learn tolerance.

The war came then. Still determined to be a poet, I made up a set of windy martial verses, and sold them to a Christmas card firm for seven and sixpence. At the same time I was working twelve hours a day for from ten to twelve shillings a week. I use that as my excuse. Printed for some reason in mauve ink, these verses had the look of weak cocoa.

At the age of twenty I wrote my autobiography in fifty thousand words. I still have it. It amazes me by its arrogance. All I was not I put in that autobiography. Then I got married and went to live in France. And there I wrote a business novel, which, fortunately, fell overboard from a Channel steamer. I caught a quick view of these sheets of thick paper untidily strewing the sea, not realising that they were my novel for some time.

Then for six or seven years I wrote nothing. But that did not stop my habit of thinking. My husband and I had a small house built on the top of a hill in Yorkshire, where there was a forty-mile view from the windows. I hadn't very much to do, and I used to look out of the windows a lot at the clouds, and wish that I had half a dozen children. It was no use wishing. I hadn't. I swopped an old gramophone for a typewriter – it was, I remember, a Salter Standard – the letters of which were both broken and invisible. It was a heavy thing, but I lugged it around with me, and learned to type on it.

One day in '26 or '27, I am not sure of the year, I suddenly wrote a story straight through from beginning to end. I was absolutely amazed. I called it 'Sultan Jekker.' It was the first story I had written for a dozen years. At the age of fifteen I had written imitation Jack London, imitation Bret Harte, imitation anybody-who-took-my-fancy stories, and had them in an amateur magazine that used to be sent to my father's place to bind. But 'Sultan Jekker' was not an imitation. It was mine. I wrote it straight on to the Salter typewriter, not stopping to look at the words, which I couldn't have seen anyway.

Well, my first story was written. I showed it to my husband, and he was surprised too. We wondered what to do with it. We had not seen any of the same sort in popular magazines. But I found a different kind of magazine in the public library. It was called the *Adelphi*. I admired every contributor to this paper. There was a man called D H Lawrence, who had written two books that I had read – *Sons and Lovers,* and *Aaron's Rod.* I knew that he knew what he was talking about. He was the best contributor of all, I thought. And I thought, 'Very well, then. Go where the best is, or nowhere at all.'

All the same, I kept that story for a long time. I took it with me on a visit to London, meaning to drop it in the letter box of the *Adelphi*, which was then in Cursitor Street, Chancery Lane. I prowled about Chancery Lane every day for a week, never getting up enough courage to put it in the letter box. I took it back home with me.

Then one day I put the story into a clean envelope, enclosed a stamped envelope for return – nothing else, not a single word of writing – addressed it very simply to the editor of the *Adelphi*, and posted it. There was an uphill walk of a mile from the postbox. I went back up the hill feeling as if I had committed a kind of crime. My husband tried to console me. 'They can't do anything worse than send it back.'

On the last day of March, 1927, I got a letter. At that time I had very few correspondents, and a letter was an event. But this was in my own handwriting; I knew what it was, and did not want to open it. Of course I did open it eventually, and of course it contained my MS. There was also a note from John Middleton Murry, in his own handwriting. 'Dear Sir,' it ran, 'this is a *good* story. Unfortunately, in all human probability the *Adelphi* will be coming to an end after two more numbers, and I am therefore unable to accept it. If, however, you still find the *Adelphi* being published after June next, send your story to me again.'

I believe I could have walked straight off the cliff at the end of the garden, across to the moor top at the other side of the valley without going anywhere near the ground. Such was the effect of these words on me.

I waited to see if the *Adelphi* came out in September. But all the meantime I was writing away like one possessed. I wrote story after story in a trance. Very often they were badly worded. I was unable to get them right. Many of the stories in my first book I re-wrote from ten to fifteen times. 'Frost in April' I typed out eighteen times. Quite boldly I sent a tale to a weekly called the *Outlook*. It was taken and printed, and paid for, too, but I hardly noticed it, so hungrily was I waiting for the *Adelphi* to reappear.

In the September it did come out again, and within eighteen months at least five of my stories had appeared in the *Adelphi* – there and nowhere else. I don't believe I sent them anywhere else. I had no other desire than to be with this rich company of writers.

At that time Mr John W Coulter was assistant editor. He was the first writing man I had ever met, and I thought he was half a god. I went with my husband to that office in Cursitor Street, and Mr Coulter thought that my husband was the writer, and talked to him all the time. We were on our way to Spain, and had our luggage with us. My husband is, above all, a businessman, and knows more about the structure of cloth than about books. He was getting in a literary fog, saying yes and no in the wrong places, when I jumped up and said miserably, 'Look here, I wrote those stories.' I can still see Mr Coulter, looking like a schoolmaster behind a desk, with the two of us sitting in front of him like a couple of Will Hay's scholars.

On our return, Mr Murry wrote to say that if I had enough stories for a volume he would do his best, though he could not promise anything, to help me place them with some publisher.

There it was. I didn't have to ask anybody for a thing. It just happened.

One day in March 1929 I went up to meet Mr Murry himself. There was to be a luncheon at some restaurant, and I was asked to go. I was much too frightened to go. I was not used to eating in front of strangers, and did not want to choke. So I went merely to have coffee.

The place was up some stairs. There seemed to be a lot of people, but I only remember Mr Murry, Mr Coulter, Sir

Richard Rees, and Dr James Young. I asked the latter if he was *the* Dr Jung, and he said no, a little coldly. My hands trembled so much that I could not lift my coffee-cup. Somebody – I believe it was Dr Young – made me take some wine, and I had alternate drinks of coffee and wine until I came round. They have told me since that they were all much more scared than I was, and I can believe it now.

When I had been there a few minutes I handed my bundle of MSS to Mr Murry, saying briefly, 'I've brought these.' He had a case, and I had not. He put them in this case, oh so casually, and I hoped he would look after them, as I had not a whole copy of any story; but I am sure that, if he had lost them, I should have been able to write them all again by heart.

However, he kept them most carefully, and sent them to Mr Jonathan Cape. At his place they were read by Mr Edward Garnett, who wrote and told me that he, too, liked them. The next thing that happened to me was the signing of an agreement, and, a month or two after that, the arrival of some proofs. By now I was getting used to amazing things. On October 14, 1929, out came my first volume of stories, *Frost in April*. And then, for weeks, nothing else happened.

My first reviewer was Humbert Wolfe. He was taking Gerald Gould's page in the Sunday *Observer,* while Mr Gould was on holiday. Mr Wolfe was not sure. He sniffed gingerly round my stories. I do not remember his exact words, but he said of one of them that it was 'like a piece of fog cut out and preserved.' I was genuinely pleased with such unique criticism.

Then the late Mr Arnold Bennett gave me half a column in the *Evening Standard*, and for a week or two my name seemed to be in every paper I picked up. I was surprised to discover that I was a printed genius. There was only one dissentient voice. Somebody in the north of Ireland sneered at 'this boy's lemonade masquerading as man's wine.' Nearly everybody called me 'he' because of my biblical name.

Now there are four volumes with my name on the cover. If Mr Murry had not troubled to write to me about that first story, I should have gone on writing, because I could not have helped it. I might have returned to my childish habit of burning everything. Then there might have been a little less work for printers, binders, booksellers; a little less wearying of eyesight, and tongue, and brain. But none of us would have been any wiser, or any more ignorant, than we are now.

Malachi Whitaker
in *Beginnings* (1935) ed. L A G Strong

AFTERWORD II

Malachi Whitaker's first published story appeared in July 1927 in *The Outlook*, a weekly periodical of 'Politics, Life, Letters and the Arts'. She was 31.

It is about Mrs Dokes, 'a big, pale, nervous woman, with a bosom like an arrested waterfall' who is regularly beaten up by her undersized husband until, encouraged by her neighbour, she pushes him into the fire. Originally called 'Mrs Dokes and Mrs Barras', the story was reprinted as 'The Paragon' in her second collection *No Luggage* (1930),

In its central scheme of two rival women pitted against a bullying man, its physicality and comic exuberance, it echoes the brutal navvy and his two warring concubines in 'Sultan Jekker', the first story she wrote; while the woman-on-man violence of its climactic scene anticipates the unexpected ending of 'Mrs Creech of Redemouth'. Though she would not have termed herself a 'feminist', Malachi's stories frequently dealt with what is gained and what is lost when women challenge their traditional roles – with unpredictable consequences that may result in triumph, or in tragedy.

On the same page as a recipe for gooseberry jam and a poem by 'the Hon. Eleanour Norton', the story's publication in *The Outlook* gave her little satisfaction – though she did enjoy the cheque. Her second publication – in the *Adelphi* in March 1928 – was the one she had been waiting for. Its contributors were very different from *The Outlook's,* and prestige and reputation, rather than remuneration, were the main rewards. Alongside D H Lawrence ('the best contributor of all, I thought'), writers between 1923 and 1948 included Katherine Mansfield, Aldous Huxley, Robert Graves, H E Bates, W H Auden, T S Eliot and Dylan Thomas. What happened initially to Malachi's first completed story 'Sultan Jekker' is unknown. Although submitted to the *Adelphi* it was not published there or in *The Outlook* but appeared in her first collection, *Frost in April,* in 1929. Instead Murry chose 'Unleashed', a story set in a Yorkshire bookbinding workshop not unlike the one owned by Malachi's father where, after leaving the much-hated Belle Vue Girl's School in Bradford, aged 13 – upon which her first act was to 'burn all my exercise books in a sort of mad frenzy' – she had worked a 53-hour week.

Over the next seven years the *Adelphi* published a further ten pieces: the last two in 1934 and 1935 were the lyrical 'Honeymoon', which experimented with the themes of love and class mobility, and 'Two Poems' – an unusual departure for Malachi. By this time Jonathan Cape had published her four acclaimed books of short stories. The writing frenzy she describes in *Beginning*s lasted until 1934 and it was over these seven years that she produced the bulk of her opus, a total of

78 out of the 94 published stories, memoir pieces, articles and poems thus far uncovered. The 78 stories appeared in her four collections: *Frost in April* (1929), *No Luggage* (1930), *Five for Silver* (1932) and *Honeymoon & Other Stories* (1934). Many were also printed separately on the literary pages of news-papers and magazines.

It was the legendary literary talent scout and editor Edward Garnett who was instrumental in recommending Malachi Whitaker to Jonathan Cape. Described by H E Bates as 'an extremely large and forbidding figure' with 'the beauty, roughly, of a grizzly bear', Garnett was credited with being the first to spot Joseph Conrad, D H Lawrence and John Galsworthy, as well as Bates himself. Cape rarely published anything without a good word from the great man, whose generosity towards new authors was well-known. In his ear-liest extant letter to Malachi, Garnett said he had been asked to write a review of *Frost in April* for *Now & Then,* Jonathan Cape's occasional periodical of 'Books & Personalities', which duly appeared in Autumn 1929. The review concluded, encouragingly: 'That her characters are just common people, as in "Brother W"... gives one hope that she will go on dipping her hand into the inexhaustible well of life and bringing out what none of us could have found for ourselves.' (Four years later Garnett used 'Prodigal's Holiday' as well as four other stories in a volume of short stories he edited called *Capajon*.)

A second letter from Edward Garnett recommended that Malachi send a story to the *Manchester Guardian*, mentioning 'that I suggested you doing so'. A new story, 'Faint Prestige', was duly printed in October 1929, the month that her first collection appeared. Succinct, poignant and witty, it concerns a 'common' but proud old man who feeds his last bag of buns to his neighbour's dog when its haughty owner cries out: 'He's got nowt for yer'. However, not all of Malachi's early reviews were quite so positive and like Murry and his assistant editor, the Irish-Canadian playwright John Coulter, most critics assumed that she was male.

Ignoring Edward Garnett's article in *Now & Then*, Malachi claimed in *Beginnings* that the first review of *Frost in April* was by the Bradford Grammar School and Oxford-educated novelist and poet Humbert Wolfe. It appeared a week after 'Faint Prestige', again in the *Manchester Guardian*. Wolfe did, indeed, sniff 'gingerly' round her stories, claiming that 'Mr Whitaker' 'has chiselled away and away till he leaves behind the sharp outline of a life utterly vague', as if by ridding her sentences of extraneous details and words, she had rendered them essentially meaningless. A second review in the *Manchester Guardian* came out a month later: by the Durham-born playwright and critic Allan Noble Monkhouse, it was even more damning and smacked of downright snobbery. 'He shows us primitive, untutored people,' says Monkhouse, singling out 'Brother W' for special condemnation, in contrast to Garnett's earlier praise: 'We must not be surprised at . . . a man who imposes his mood on life to the extent of sharing a bed with his brother for twenty years without speaking to him. Art is not to be constrained nowadays by credibility, but the incredible may be trying to the reader's indigestion.'

This charge of absurdity, or lack of credibility, is one that occurs again and again in critiques of Malachi's work – though many reviewers see this essential unpredictability, bordering on surreality, as a strength. 'I have no imagination; all my stories are *true*,' Malachi told her son, Michael Whitaker. This did not mean that they were all autobiographical, or based on her own family (although some of them were). Her material often came from first-hand observation. An instinctive musician, she could play a variety of instruments by ear and would initiate spontaneous sing-songs in pubs, bashing out music hall classics on the piano; afterwards, she would talk to those who had gathered around her, drawing out their stories, and altering them slightly. As Mark Twain said: 'Truth is stranger than Fiction . . . because Fiction is obliged to stick to possibilities. Truth isn't.'

The lukewarm reviews had little impact: Malachi was on a roll and nothing could stop her now. In any case, her critical reputation was saved by the novelist Arnold Bennett, the most influential reviewer of the time: his broad-minded column in the *Evening Standard* was read by a vast public across the UK. Published in the autumn of 1929, Bennett's review of *Frost in April* takes up about one fifth (not one half as Malachi claimed) of his column space. 'I incline to the view that Malachi is a woman,' he writes, 'but I am by no means sure.' However, there is nothing uncertain about his views of her ability: 'Made up of the common daily stuff or small beer of existence . . . the book is very fine. . . These chiefly sad stories, in addition to being thoroughly well observed, and well done in the technical sense, have strong originality, much beauty, and much emotional power. Yet their tone is very quiet indeed . . . "The Journey Home" narrates a railway accident in a manner new in fiction . . . Malachi Whitaker has quite unusual talent. And no habitual reader of fiction can afford to ignore him – or her.'

Malachi's tale of her career in *Beginnings* stops roughly here, but this was far from the end of the story. More encouraging reviews were to follow. In general, author-critics loved her. In November 1929 Vita Sackville-West reviewed *Frost in April* for the *Spectator*, declaring: 'The same economy, the same honesty, the same refusal of effective tricks, and the same determination to make each word do the duty required of it, are common to both Katherine Mansfield . . . and to Malachi Whitaker.' A year later the *Spectator* ran another positive review of Malachi's second collection, by V S Pritchett: 'She goes straight to the point in her first paragraph,' he wrote. 'Her intuitions are exact but kind, and she leaves stories "open" at the ends, without leaving them in the air.'

From mid 1929 onwards Malachi began to receive fan letters from illustrious writers. She was particularly pleased with a letter from John Galsworthy, whom she later visited: 'I thought [the stories] showed most admirable powers and a wonderfully sure touch.' Malachi called this 'the Prize Letter'. It was confirmation that she had 'arrived'.

In the autumn of 1929 H E Bates sent the first of 47 letters and cards (preserved in the West Yorkshire Archive at Bradford) to Malachi, whom he had not yet met. The son of a Northamptonshire boot factory employee and ten years her junior, he had already published two novels with Jonathan

Cape as well as numerous short stories in literary periodicals; he became her self-appointed 'mentor', which she accepted readily. From the first, his communications were filled with practical tips on potential markets, fees, how to overcome the literary world's inherent snobbery – and agents ('Don't have an agent! Oh! For God's sake. No . . . They're a race of parasitic imposters!'). He took her to lunch with Edward Garnett and introduced her to Charles Lahr's Progressive Bookshop – a meeting place for left-leaning writers in Red Lion Street in Bloomsbury. He encouraged her to send a story to the *New Statesman*: 'The Comedian' – about a young man who realises his chosen career path does not suit him – was subsequently published in March 1930. He regularly reviewed her work, wrote to her ('"Honeymoon" is the most perfect thing . . . so damned warm and genuine') and in 1934 published 'The White Line' in a volume he edited called *New Stories*. He also prompted her to demand a £10 fee per story from *John O'London's Weekly*, the popular news and culture weekly ('Bleed him, yes, you must bleed him!' he wrote).

John O' London's Weekly and Charles Lahr's Bookshop were each to play a large role in Malachi's literary life. She never did make it into what Bates termed the 'snob-pit' of high-paying magazines like *Good Housekeeping*, and the American market proved elusive, but, from 1930-40, twenty of her stories appeared in *JOLW*, including six reprinted here ('The End of the Queue', 'The Lonely One', 'Spring Day at Slater's End', 'Pin's Fee Wife', 'For a Small Moment' and 'Salem Street'). From 1928 the Acting Editor, later Editor, of *JOLW* was Frank Whitaker (no relation), a Yorkshireman who had attended Keighley Boys' Grammar School and became a good friend to Malachi. In its heyday, *JOLW* had a circulation of 80,000 and aimed to make literary culture accessible to everyone – from the highbrow to the self-educated working man. In its choice of short fiction, the magazine tended towards the traditional – which may have limited Malachi's experiments in form, though it provided a reliable platform for her work.

Not surprisingly, given Frank Whitaker's origins, the journal dedicated many column inches to Yorkshire. Regular contributors included J B Priestley (Bradford) and Phyllis Bentley (Halifax), while novels by Storm Jameson (Whitby), Winifred Holtby (Rudston, near Hull) and Lettice Cooper (Leeds) were given detailed reviews. However, Malachi did not feel a part of this 'Yorkshire coterie'. Lettice Cooper reviewed her work very positively for the *Yorkshire Post* on at least one occasion, but Malachi had little time for Phyllis Bentley, and seems to have had no personal connection with either Storm Jameson or Winifred Holtby who, like Phyllis Bentley, were both university-educated and born into well-off Yorkshire families. Malachi certainly met up with J B Priestley, the son of a Bradford schoolmaster, who wrote to her after favourably reviewing one of her books, but the two apparently fell out over politics during a lunch at Bradford's Midland Hotel, as Malachi's views had shifted towards to the centre and Priestley's remained firmly on the left. Yet, in 1972, Priestley wrote an extremely kind letter to Malachi, saying how sad it was that she had given up writing, and suggesting she try her hand at a radio play.

In the 1930s Malachi made far more friends at the Progressive Bookshop – run by the sandal-wearing, German-born anarchist Charles Lahr. Here she met a whole circle of non-Bloomsbury, Social Realist artists and authors, including the short story writer Gerald Kersh and the novelist, diarist, Mass Observation researcher and, later, mystic, Gay Taylor ('Loran Hurnscot'). Born in Pontefract, Yorkshire, Taylor and Malachi became lifelong friends. For a while they shared a flat near the bookshop, where Malachi stayed whenever she was in London (both were destroyed in the Second World War); and although they had their ups and downs, each wrote around 600 letters to the other over the years.

After the publication of *Honeymoon, & Other Stories* in 1934, Malachi's inspiration began to sputter and her output slowed down. This coincided with the adoption of her two children, Michael and Valerie, who gave an alternative focus to her life. It also coincided with the family's move to Bolton Old Hall, a grand Yorkshire manor of which Malachi writes in her memoir *And So Did I*: 'I have my room in the new part, which was run up in front of the old house in sixteen hundred and twenty-seven.' The house was a two-minute walk from the much less grand Clara Road, Wrose (on the outskirts of Bradford), where Malachi was born, and moving in repre-sented quite a coup; for a while, she harboured hopes that this was to be her final home, but following the family's usual pattern (Malachi lived at thirty-eight addresses over the course of her restless life) they moved out in 1943, only to move back in again for a couple of years in 1946.

In *And So Did I*, she also reports that 'for three years I had written no stories'. Technically, this was true, but she was being disingenuous. In 1934 at least three new stories were printed, although two of them were very slight. In 1935 came the two poems in the *Adelphi*, while in 1937 the Cresset Press published Malachi and Gay Taylor's anonymous spoof novel, *The Autobiography of Ethel Firebrace*: this purported to be the memoir of a 'famous' novelist, with chapter headings including 'Walls That Have Known Me' and 'My Psychic Experiences'. Michael Whitaker remembers his mother and Gay Taylor bolting the door to the library at Bolton Old Hall and peals of laughter issuing from the room.

In 1938, two stories came out in *John O'London's Weekly* and, in 1939, *And So Did I* appeared. At least six more stories, memoir pieces and a book review were published in the 1940s, mainly in *JOLW* and *The Listener*, before Malachi went out in a blaze of glory in 1946 with 'The Mandoline', printed in the periodical *Selected Stories*, edited by Reginald Moore. The story of a young German prisoner of war who befriends an old Yorkshire couple after borrowing their dead soldier son's mandoline, it was broadcast in several languages on the radio. After that there were two compilations of previously published stories, both confusingly entitled *Selected Stories* (Maurice Fridberg, 1946; and Jonathan Cape, 1949) – and then no more. After her death, there was a 1984 selection called *The Crystal Fountain and Other Stories* and now, thirty-three years later, this Persephone selection.

Malachi spent the remaining twenty-eight years of her life travelling, reading, learning to play different musical instruments, including a drum set and the Hawaiian guitar, writing hundreds of letters – and, of course, moving house, endlessly.

Some time during the 1940s she told her family, 'I'm all written out'. The reasons why her inspiration dried up are complex. A highly instinctive writer, perhaps the change in social status, after her (by now) mill-owning husband began to make money, removed her from the working and lower middle-class Yorkshire milieu she felt most comfortable writing about; and, of course, tastes and fashions changed radically after the Second World War. The mixed reviews she received for *And So Did I* may also have had an impact. Once again the *Manchester Guardian* was surprisingly negative, publishing a review straight out of Bates's 'snob-pit' by a critic known as 'MC': 'This is a book that shows a somewhat naive mind,' wrote 'MC'. 'Most of its small talk is agreeable enough in a desultory way, but many of the general reflections strike one as being neither worth making nor worth reading.' The *Spectator* agreed, saying the book was 'a dangerous attempt to make new ground' and that 'Mrs Malachi Whitaker's . . . thoughts and feelings are dull.' Fortunately, the *New Statesman*, the *Listener* and the ever-loyal *John O' London's Weekly* were all positive, while Stevie Smith used the book as inspiration for a poem in *Now & Then*. With its quirky rhymes and line-breaks, the second stanza captures the filmic feel of a Malachi story, in miniature:

'The writing is like a talky
Interrupted by a door-key
Turning, a kettle boiling,
A child swinging on a loose railing.'

A clue from a characteristically sparky article Malachi published in *John O' London's Weekly* on 28 July 1939 may be more relevant. Entitled 'I Could Not Miss a Word of Rider Haggard', it is about 'books I cannot forget', including the works of Emily Bronte. '*Wuthering Heights* made the greatest impression the work of a woman has ever made on me. I respect and admire a woman who can keep her mouth shut when she has nothing to say, and above everything Emily Bronte did that.'

Or perhaps Malachi simply wished to be forgotten; although there are hints that this may not be the case.

Many of her stories are, fundamentally, about shifting social positions and identities as men, and especially women, challenge their status, assigned roles and social class in a society in flux between the wars. A searching, restless soul, Malachi's own insecurity about these issues was balanced, at times, by a deep and driving faith in her ability; at some profound level perhaps she recognised her own exceptionality.

The quotation on the frontispiece of *And So Did I,* from Coleridge's *Ancient Mariner,* provides a further clue. Self-effacing and witty as ever, she sees a parallel between herself and the thousands of unremarkable, viscous creatures who populate this earth; and yet, buried far below, the hope seems to linger that she may not entirely be forgotten:

'And a thousand thousand slimy things
Lived on; and so did I.'

Valerie Waterhouse,
Milan, 2017